HORROR STORIES FOR CHILDREN:

(a.k.a. Life Lessons for Adults)

by

Robert Rahula

© 2017 Robert Rahula

robertrahula.com

facebook.com/robert.rahula

ALSO BY ROBERT RAHULA

NOVELS:

Messieurs
Panamaniac
Island of Misfits
Day Another Paradise In
One Last Fling
Bathhouse Stories
Conversation in a Belgian Bar
All the Yage in Reno
Exigent Circumstances

POETRY:

Trigger Points
Dentro Del Corazón Bloqueada
Camino
Migration
I Sing the Body Politic
Wonderland
From Whose Bourn
Poemas Españoles
Expat Poems

ANTHOLOGIES:

Half Life
The Essential Dan Landes

HORROR STORIES FOR CHILDREN:

(a.k.a. *Life Lessons for Adults*)

by

Robert Rahula

WARNING:

DESPITE THE TITLE, THIS IS NOT A BOOK FOR
CHILDREN. THIS IS A BOOK FOR ADULTS.
DO NOT GIVE THIS BOOK TO CHILDREN.

Alma-gator Press

Barcelona • Madrid • La Chorrera

Horror Stories for Children
(a.k.a. Life Lessons for Adults)
© 2017 by Robert Rahula

This is a work of fiction. Characters, organizations, businesses, products, locales, and events portrayed in this book either are products of the author's imagination or are used fictitiously.

First Printing, 2017

ISBN 978-0-9994736-0-3

Alma-Gator Press
Barcelona • Madrid • La Chorrera

For Mary

Table of Contents

HOW TO POLYGRAPH A FROG

Polygraphing a frog is not that different from polygraphing a human. In some ways, it's easier, because it does not matter where you attach the electrodes. However, getting the electrodes to stick *is* a problem, due to the frog's slimy skin. I have found that duct tape works best. Simply apply *all* of the electrodes to a large piece of duct tape first, then wrap the frog entirely in the duct tape. This also helps prevent the frog from hopping around during questioning.

Once the electrodes are applied, you need to get a base level reading. The base level reading is defined simply as whatever the electrodes pick up. Sometimes with frogs you can get a reading on respiration...sometimes pulse...sometimes blood pressure—if you're lucky—but never skin conductivity, because of the aforementioned slime. So whatever measure you detect when you first start, that measure will do as your base level reading.

Once you've got your base level reading, you need to determine your "lie threshold." The lie threshold is how much your base level reading changes when the frog is lying. Because of the scientific fact that blood pressure, respiration, and pulse rates increase at exactly the same rate with lying as with the emotion of fear, the way to get your lie threshold reading is to induce fear in the frog. I usually do this with a small 12-volt shock.

This is where the duct tape comes in handy—allowing you to easily hold the frog while you apply the shock. Wear rubber gloves, of course. Once the shock is applied, you will see your base level reading shoot up. Mark that upper limit with a red pen. That is your lie threshold.

Now, you have to calm your frog back down before you can begin questioning. I usually offer the frog some birthday cake, preferably a piece with plenty of icing. Frogs are particularly keen on birthday cake, especially if it is their birthday. I always tell them it's their birthday when I serve them the cake.

Once your frog has calmed down and your readings are back down to the base level, you can begin the questioning. Unlike with human subjects, you don't have to start off with easy questions, because you don't need to establish a base level reading—you already have that. So you can start off with tough questions.

"Where were you last Saturday night?"

"What happened to my car keys?"

"Who's been here while I've been gone?"

Now, of course, you're not looking for a verbal response... obviously...because frogs can't talk. Any idiot knows that. But what you are looking for is sudden electrode activity— something that approaches the lie threshold. Then you can narrow in on the guilty subject area.

Suppose, for example, you see an increase in respiration with the question "Who's been here while I've been gone?" Then you can start in with specific questions.

"Has Jason been over while I was at work?"

"Was it somebody else?"

"Was it Mark?"

"Did my wife seem excited to see him?"

"Did they go into the bedroom?"

Usually, by trial and error, you can get the frog to tell you everything it has seen.

This comes in very useful later when trying to entrap the wife in casual conversation, such as, "Have you seen Mark lately? No? Really? I heard he came by. No, a friend told me."

One piece of advice: Never tell your wife where you got the information. Frogs are the absolute best informants because people never notice them sitting quietly in the corner of the room, watching everything.

THE TROUBLE WITH SUPERPOWERS

The trouble with superpowers is that they have limits. Say, for example, you've been beamed up to an alien space-ship, and the eight-foot-tall, green lizard-like scary-looking (but actually beneficent) alien is allowing you to choose one (but only one) superpower from a table of superpowers. Maybe it's a table covered with different rings—you know, like Green Lantern's ring—and each one has a specific superpower. And you can choose any one that you want.

Well, of course you immediately think of that young woman Shirley, who lives in the same apartment building as you, and so you say, "I'd like the ring that makes me invisible"—thinking it would be nice to take a peek at her in the shower...

Or maybe you're not quite so sexually perverted, but you still say, "I'd like the ring that makes me invisible"—thinking you might sneak around Congressional offices and slit some throats—you know, to help make the country a better place and all.

Well, wait a minute...not so fast. What if the ring makes

you invisible, but not your clothes? Not so undetectable, unless you like prancing totally naked through the air-conditioned halls of Congress. And what if you had a sandwich for lunch? Would *that* be visible in your stomach? After all, it's not "part of you" until it's digested. And speaking of digestion, what about all your poop? Would that be visible even if *you* were invisible, since that poop is really just undigested food and not you? And what about those metal fillings in your teeth? Wouldn't they be visible even if your flesh was invisible? Or those heart stents? Can you imagine Shirley stepping out of the shower and seeing a bundle of poopy intestines, two heart stents, and a mouthful of fillings grinning at her? And by the way, if you've got heart stents, aren't you kind of too old to be sneaking naked into young women's bathrooms?

And what about permanency? Even if the magic ring makes you *and* your clothes *and* your fillings *and* your food *and* your poop *and* your stents invisible, can you revert back to being visible? How does that work? Do you just take off the ring? Or is it like all other forms of corruption: once corrupt, always corrupt? Being invisible for an hour is fun—but being invisible the rest of your life is another story.

The point is, when dealing with aliens bearing gifts of superpowers, you've got to be specific! You've got to read the small print. Ask Superman—that kryptonite shit hurts!

"Okay," you say, "forget invisibility. I want to be able to fly." A pragmatic choice, given the hassle of dealing with TSA agents. But again, how exactly are you flying? Have you ever tried lying on your stomach on the floor and pretending you can fly and holding your head up so you can see where the fuck you're going? It hurts to hold your head up like that. Any flight longer than ten minutes and you are going to have horrible neck cramps. And how fast are you flying? Do you need a helmet? Do you have to watch out for birds or farmers with shotguns who think you're another government drone? And speaking of government, do you know where the restricted flight areas are? Do you think you can read a map while you're flying through the air with your new superpower?

"Okay," you ask, "what about gold? What if I choose a magic ring that makes gold? Not much, maybe just an ounce a day." Well, there might be such a ring on the alien's table—one with a tiny hinge so that a portal opens up every morning at 10 a.m. and poops out several nuggets of pure gold, adding up each day to exactly one ounce. Not a bad superpower. Discrete. No problem keeping your clothes on. No need for a helmet. Another advantage of creating gold nuggets is that you could just move somewhere near any ol' mountain or rural area and claim you are a prospector. Establish a good relationship with a local gold buyer and just show up once a month with about two pounds of gold and collect your cash. And let's say that gold stays between $1250 and $1300 an ounce—that means that your superpower would be "creating" about $37,500 a month in gold nuggets. And you could simply offer to buy Shirley a new car if she'd let you watch her in the shower...or you could simply save up your money and buy a Congressman and help make the country a better place and all.

But you know...even the gold-making superpower has its limits. First of all, you've got to make sure that every morning at 10 a.m. there's no one around to see your magic ring making gold. No matter how much Shirley likes the new car you gave her, once she sees that tiny door on your ring pop open and gold nuggets start pooping out, she'll be spiking your drink and yanking that ring off your hand and disappearing into the night. Also, while everyone thinks that gold never loses its value...the fact is, you can't buy enough Congressmen to prevent the next nuclear war from destroying our entire world economic system, and then the only thing of value will be food, water, and ammunition. Nobody will want your gold. Your gold-pooping ring won't be worth shit.

The fact is—for any superpower you can think of, there is a situation that can arise—or will arise—that makes that superpower completely useless. It's true. Make a list of superpowers on the left side of the page and then see how fast you can fill the right side of the page with some situation that works against it.

"Okay," you say. "I get the point. Maybe I'll ask for a superpower that just allows me to help others. What if my superpower is healing the lame and making the blind see again?"

Well...remember what happened to the last guy who had that superpower?

No, the fact is, there is no superpower that doesn't have a downside. Take me for example. A few decades back, a giant alien flying saucer beamed me up and an eight-foot-tall, green, lizard-like alien asked me what superpower I wanted. And I told him that I wanted to be a writer. And so I've been doing that for the last few decades. But I didn't read the small print. I wasn't specific. I forgot to say *best-selling* writer. So now I sit in front of my computer screen every day while my superpowers poop all over the page. I'm a very prolific writer. Whoop-deee-doo. Every superpower has its limits.

HOW TO FEED A HUNGRY BEAR

I woke up because Nuzzle the Bear was poking my face with his wet nose. Nuzzle always sleeps with me, but he usually sleeps way past the time I get up. But this morning he was deliberately waking me up with his wet nose and his hot breath.

"What is it?" I asked him, irritably.

"I'm hungry," he said.

"Go back to sleep," I said.

"I'm hungry," he said again.

When Nuzzle first came to live with me, he was very cute. He was just a small bear cub then. I could pick him up with one hand. He loved to nuzzle with me, so I named him Nuzzle. He liked to sleep with me too, and for the first year it was fun. But now he's three hundred pounds and takes up most of the bed. And his claws! Jesus Palomino! You think you have problems when your husband or wife doesn't clip their toenails? Think what 4-inch bear claws can do to your back!

Which was exactly what happened this morning.

"Eeee-ouch!" I screamed as Nuzzle raked his claws across my back, drawing blood.

"Oh sorry," he said, "but I'm hungry."

"Can't you clip those?" I yelled, climbing out of the bed.

"I said I was sorry," Nuzzle answered.

I went over and stood in front of the full length mirror on the bathroom door and twisted around to look at my back. It looked like I'd been crawling—unsuccessfully—under barbed wire. Thin lines of blood were running down my back.

"Look at this!" I said. "Why aren't you wearing those gloves I bought you?"

"They're too hot," Nuzzle said.

"Jeez," I said. I poured some hydrogen peroxide on a paper towel and tried to wipe the scratches, but I couldn't reach all of them.

"Did I mention I was hungry?" Nuzzle asked.

"Several times," I replied.

"Well?" he asked.

"Okay, okay, I'll hop down to the pastry shop and get some bear claws for you," I said.

"That's not funny," he replied.

"Well, what do you want?" I asked.

"Pancakes with honey," he said.

"We're out of honey," I said. "What's your second choice?"

"Waffles with honey," he said.

"Jeez...I'll see what I can do," I said, and started to get dressed.

Luckily, I found two extra jars of honey in the back of one of the kitchen cupboards. A good thing, because (a) I didn't feel like driving my car with my back all scratched up and bleeding, and (b) I certainly wasn't going to take Nuzzle back to IHOP again. No siree, not after the last time.

"Good news," I called up to the bedroom. "You're getting pancakes."

"Yay," he shouted. "Holler when they're ready."

So anyway, that's how you feed a hungry bear—you make him pancakes. But that's not the point of the story. The point of this story is the nature of evil. But if I had entitled the story "The Nature of Evil," you wouldn't have started to read it, would you? So here's what happened: I cooked up a big pile of pancakes—like 50 or so— and called up to Nuzzle that they were ready, and he lumbered down to the kitchen table and sat down, and while he was chowing down, we had the following conversation.

"So I've been thinking about the nature of evil," he said.

"Really?" I asked, "And what are your thoughts on it?"

"Well, I think it exists," he said.

"That's not very profound," I said.

"Oh, yes it is," he said. "A lot of people don't think it exists. Buddhists, for example—they don't think evil exists; they just think it's ignorance— you know, blindness to the way things work, attachment to desire, thinking only of oneself, not understanding the true consequence of wrongful thought."

"Buddhists don't believe in evil?" I asked

"Not in the way you Christians believe in it," Nuzzle said.

"You've got honey on your chin," I said. "And I'm not exactly Christian."

"You're close enough," he said, wiping his chin.

"So what do the Buddhists believe?" I asked.

"Well, they talk about the ignorant mind, or the impure mind, polluted with false thoughts because of attachment. In the Dhammapada, Buddha says that all action follows thought, and that if a person speaks or acts from impure thoughts, suffering will follow him, the way the wheels of an oxcart follow the ox."

"Hmmph," I said, "when Christians talk about impure thoughts, they always mean sex."

"Yes, I know. I've never liked that translation—'impure

mind'—I prefer 'ignorant mind', or as we bears say, 'human mind'. But anyway, the emphasis in Buddhism is on how suffering inevitably follows ignorant thoughts or actions. Christians, on the other hand, always assume that people are getting away with evil, so they have to be caught and punished–made to suffer–because otherwise they would never be held accountable for their actions."

"I've never liked that expression," I said. "To hold someone accountable...Whenever I hear someone say that, I know what they really mean is they want to take their revenge on that person."

"Yes," Nuzzle said. "And speaking of revenge, did you know that Nietzsche said that the basis of law *is* revenge? Can you pass the butter please?"

"Here you go. Yes, I did know that. Did you know that Nietzsche had syphilis from visiting prostitutes?"

"I did know that," Nuzzle said. "Did you know that bears can't get syphilis?"

"Really?" I said. "No, I didn't know that."

"Anyway," Nuzzle said, "back to evil. So, the Buddhists don't think that people are evil—but that they are ignorant. Most bears are Buddhists, by the way. But you Christians— you think evil people exist. You all have Satan, the Devil, Beelzebub, the Evil One, etcetera, all waiting to take over people."

"Well," I said, "it explains a lot of things. It certainly makes it easier to tell Bible stories. You know, 'such and such people were evil, so God drowned them in a big flood'—and it makes raising children a lot easier too. You just teach them that the world is divided into good and evil, and if they do evil, they get spanked. Besides, it just seems so obvious, when you look at the world. Some politician gets elected, then he starts embezzling money, and then somebody finds out and is going to blow the whistle and expose him, so the politician hires a hitman, and then the whole thing blows up, and the politician goes to jail. He seems evil. He acts evil. It all just looks evil."

"Yeah," Nuzzle said. "I don't go with that theory."

"But I thought you said that you believe evil exists," I said.

"I do," Nuzzle said, "but I don't think what you just described was evil. That was just someone being ignorant, like the Buddhists say. That politician was just deluded that power and money were things to be desired, and his beliefs led him to do certain actions,   and—like the wheels of the oxcart following the ox—his ignorant actions landed him in trouble. But evil is something else."

"What is it then?" I asked.

"Well," Nuzzle said, sticking his fork into the last stack of pancakes from the platter and moving them over to his plate, "you know how the subatomic world has the strong force and the weak force?"

"No," I said.

"Okay," he said, "how about gravity and anti-gravity?"

"Well, I've heard of it," I said, "but does anti-gravity really exist?"

"Of course," Nuzzle said. "My point is that, in nature, there is always the appearance of duality. You know, for every action there is an equal and opposite reaction, and all that. Sine waves go up, then down. There's energy and entropy, order and chaos. Anyway, my point is, these are all forces. Evil is just a force, like chaos. It's just another force in the universe."

"Well," I said, feeling a bit exasperated, "how is that different from the Christian belief that there's a force called evil?"

"It's different because the force I'm describing is not evil," Nuzzle said.

"What? What is it then?"

"Well, it's evil but it's not evil—it's just a force," Nuzzle explained. "Look, if a tornado blows your house down, you don't think it's evil, do you?"

"No," I said, "bad luck maybe, but not evil."

"What if the contractor who built the house used shoddy materials, didn't follow code, didn't build your house right, and all the other houses in the neighborhood were not affected by the tornado, except yours, because of this contractor?" Nuzzle asked.

"Well, I would say he was evil," I replied.

"But not the tornado?" Nuzzle asked.

"No, the tornado was just a force of nature," I said.

"Okay, what if the contractor and the tornado were the same force," Nuzzle asked, "somehow working together...not conspiring, but simply part of the same combination of events that resulted in your house being blown away?"

"Well, Nuzzle," I said, "this is just one of those Zen koans, isn't it? Like, good can't exist without evil, life can't exist without death, yada yada yada."

"Maybe," he said. "Are there any more pancakes?"

"No. You ate them all," I said.

"I'm still hungry. Can we go to IHOP?"

"Absolutely not," I said.

"Why not?"

"Why not?!" I exclaimed. "Remember last week when you mauled that waiter's arm off? We've been banned from IHOP! We can never go back there!"

"Well, he was being an asshole," Nuzzle said.

"Really? What happened to your theory about there being no evil people?" I asked.

"Well, I'm just a bear. You don't fuck with bears. He was being an asshole."

"So you tore his arm off?"

"Yeah."

"Not very Christian of you," I said.

"I'm not Christian."

"Not very Buddhist of you."

"Yeah, probably not, but it was very bearish of me. I can't help it—I'm just another force of nature. And I'm still hungry."

"How 'bout some scrambled eggs?" I suggested.

Nuzzle frowned. "Is that all you got?"

"I could put some lox in them," I suggested.

"Now you're talking," Nuzzle said and smiled.

While I was getting three cartons of eggs out from the refrigerator, I asked him, "So you're saying that evil is just another force in nature?"

"Right," he said.

"And that it's not evil, but we just give it the name evil because it has unpleasant consequences for us?"

"Damn!" Nuzzle said, "You're pretty quick for a human. That's it exactly! We don't call desire *evil* even though it leads to suffering. We don't call death *evil* even though it's the worst thing ever. We understand intuitively that desire and death are just part of the process of life."

"Well, Nuzzle," I said as I was cracking eggs into a bowl, "that all sounds pretty Buddhist to me."

"Yeah, maybe it is," he admitted. "We bears have a natural affinity for Buddhism. Did I ever tell you I met the Dalai Lama one time?"

"No! Really?"

"Yup. And do you know what he said?"

"What?"

"He said, 'Holy Shit–there's a fucking bear in my room!' So I had to get out of there fast."

"You're putting me on," I said.

"Just a little," Nuzzle said.

I whipped the eggs up in a big bowl until they were frothy, and then pulled a pound of lox out of the refrigerator and started peeling off thin slices and dropping them into the eggs.

"Damn, that smells good," Nuzzle said. "I love salmon.

Why didn't you tell me you had salmon?"

"You said you wanted pancakes," I replied.

"Yeah, well I did. And they were good. Thank you. That's the nature of desire, you know. Always changing. You feed desire and it just changes into another desire."

"You're welcome. And yes, I've noticed that about desire. But you know what else I notice?" I asked.

"What?"

"That I like it," I said. "I like the feeling of desiring something, or someone. It has its own...its own sensation... its own vibration."

"Ah yes, that's true," Nuzzle said. "And so does evil. Evil has its own vibration too. We bears, we can smell it. Almost all animals can—except humans, of course. But even in your devolved state, you can still sense—intuit—when someone is evil."

"I thought you didn't believe that people were evil," I said.

"I'm using a term of speech," Nuzzle explained.

"Oh," I said, and then I asked, "So you can smell evil?"

"Uh-huh. You know how dogs always sniff people when they meet them for the first time? It's because they're trying to determine whether that person is a good person or not. If a person smells like evil, the dogs instantly hate them. We bears are even more sensitive. We don't have to get very close at all to know if someone is evil."

"Huh," I said. "Well, that makes sense...Yeah, I agree with that. When people are up to no good, they give off a vibe. I can tell when I don't trust someone."

"Yup. What you're smelling is evil," Nuzzle said.

"I don't know if I'm *smelling* it, but I certainly can feel it," I said.

"Of course you're smelling it," Nuzzle exclaimed. "What do you think intuition is? Some kind of extrasensory perception? No, it's what left of your sense of smell. You humans have lost most of that sense, all because you wanted cute little small noses. Ha! Look where that got you—cute noses and no ability to sniff out danger. No wonder so many animals turned their backs on you."

"Dogs still like us," I protested.

"Dogs are stupid," Nuzzle countered. "How are those eggs coming?"

"The first batch is almost done," I said. "So let me ask you this: If you think there are no evil people, just ignorant people, do you think they still face the consequences of their ignorant actions?"

"Ha!" Nuzzle laughed. "Spoken like a Christian! What you're really asking is: are they held accountable?"

"Well, yeah," I had to admit. I slid the first batch of scrambled eggs and lox out of the frying pan and onto a plate, and then placed the plate in front of Nuzzle. Then I poured some more egg mixture into the frying pan to make another batch.

"Accountability and suffering are not the same," Nuzzle said as he ate. "Boy, these are good. Some people get away with their misdeeds—in fact, most everyone does. No one is held accountable for all their sins, but that does not mean they don't suffer because of them."

"No ultimate judgment from God?" I asked.

"Please," Nuzzle grunted. "Don't go there. No, there is no ultimate judgment from God. That's something you Christians made up to satisfy your bloodlust to hold other people *accountable* for what you call *sins*. We bears think that is so stupid."

"What about the Buddhist bears?" I asked. "Don't they believe that if they do good in this life that they will come back in the next life as something better than a bear?"

"Something better than a bear?" Nuzzle asked. "Are you trying to insult me? There's nothing better than a bear. Something better than a bear! Ha!"

"So, bears don't believe in reincarnation?" I asked.

Nuzzle looked at me with a serious look in his eye. "Nope," he said. "This life is it."

"Then what's the point of doing good?" I asked. "I mean, if you're not held accountable in this life, and you're not held accountable in the next life, what's the point of trying to live a good life in this life?

"I'm not a philosopher," Nuzzle said. "I'm just a bear. We bears only have two rules. Number one: Suffering follows ignorant thought. Number two: Don't fuck with bears."

HOW THE LEOPARD GOT HIS SPOTS

He stole 'em! He fucking just *stole* 'em. He walked into Willy Finn's store, stuck a gun to Willy's head, and flat out stole 'em. If I'm lying, I'm dying. That leopard waltzed into that place at closing time, jacked up on PCP or DMT or STP or all three, pulled out a lil' .44, pointed it right at the middle of Willy Finn's forehead, just an inch away from skin, and said, "Word on da street is dat you gotz Spots..." Then, the leopard smiled. You ever see a leopard smile? It's a smile that'll turn your blood cold. You never want to see a leopard smile. They say the last thing a leopard does before he tears out an antelope's neck is to smile at the antelope. That's some cold-blooded shit, to smile at someone just before you kill 'em.

Well, Willy Finn knew this, so he thought he was dead. He thought he had maybe three seconds before the leopard was going to blow his brains all over the back wall. His whole life flashed in front of him—well, not his whole life...in fact, just a few seconds of his life...actually just the fact that he had just paid rent on his building that morning, had just put the check in the mail, and now he was going to die. An entire month's rent, paid for nothing. That was the only part of his life that flashed through his mind.

But somehow, Willy had the wherewithal to say to the leopard, "Yeah, I ordered your size, and I've been saving them just for you."

I guess when some people are about to die, they get an odd sense of humor. Anyway, the leopard thought it was funny, you know, the idea that Willy would order Spots in the leopard's size. I mean, what size does a leopard wear? Even the leopard didn't know what size he wore. I mean, a Spot's a Spot right? But the leopard thought it was funny, so he says, "Yeah? Where they at?"

Now Willy didn't want to make any sudden movement, on account of the leopard holding a .44 to his head, so he just jerked his eyeballs to the right and said, "They're in that box on the counter."

The box happened to be on the counter because right before the leopard walked in, Willy was about to get his pricing sheet and measuring stick out, and he was going to price those Spots. He had just opened the box. So the leopard kept his gun pointed at Willy's head but reached over and lifted the cardboard flap open, just to confirm that Willy was telling the truth. And yup, the box was full of Spots.

"Thanks," the leopard said, and he picked up the whole box and started backing out of the store, still keeping a bead on Willy's head. Willy didn't move. He just stood there with his hands in the air. But just as the leopard got to the door, for some reason, Willy shouted out, "We have a No-Return Policy." That made the leopard really laugh. The way I hear it, the leopard was going to shoot Willy, but that last joke kind of made the leopard respect Willy just a bit.

But the point is, the leopard didn't earn those Spots like he claims. And he certainly didn't inherit the Spots like his wife claims. No, he fucking stole 'em, pure and simple. If I'm lying, I'm dying.

NATURAL SELECTION

Billy walked into Castaways looking more pissy and haggard than usual. Walt noticed it as soon as Billy sat down at the bar.

"What's wrong, man?" Walt immediately asked him.

"Lost my job," Billy said as he lifted a finger to signal the barkeeper. The barkeeper walked directly over to the Blue Moon tap—Billy's usual selection of beer—and glanced over at Billy. Billy nodded, and the bartender poured him a glass.

"Bummer, man," Walt said. "Where were you working?"

"T-shirt factory downtown," Billy said.

"Didn't know we had a T-shirt factory in town," Walt said.

The barkeeper came over to Billy with the beer and the pull-tab jar. Since it was before 5:00, draft beer was only $1.75 and came with a free pull-tab. Billy pulled one out of the jar and opened it. "Not a Winner," it read. Billy handed the bartender $2.00.

"Yeah, it's down on Fourth, next to Value Village, but it's not a store. It's just an office. They only sell T-shirts online."

The barkeeper brought a quarter back and placed it on

the bar in front of Billy. Billy picked it up, wiped it against his pants to get the wetness off it, and stuck it in his pocket.

"What did you do there?" Walt asked.

"I'm the slogan-man," Billy said, "or, I was the slogan-man."

Walt gave Billy a puzzled look.

"I made up slogans to put on the front of the T-shirts," Billy explained. "You know—cute sayings, funny lines, quips, quotes."

"Really?" said Walt. "That must have been a fun job."

"No, it was crap. I really hated it. It was so boring."

"Really? I would have thought it would be creative."

"Nah, we used a slogan generator. I just sat in front of a computer all day."

"What's a slogan generator?" Walt asked.

"It's an app that generates slogans," Billy explained. "You can download one for free for your phone. We used a commercial one, so it was more powerful, but basically, you type in a word and the App generates hundreds of slogans that use that word."

Walt put his beer down and looked at Billy. He didn't really care for Billy, but he had never heard of a slogan generator before and this interested him.

"So," he asked, "how does that actually work?"

"Well, I'd show up in the morning, sit at my desk for about ten minutes, think up about thirty different random words, type them into the app, and it would generate about two thousand slogans. I'd read through them, highlight the ones I thought were funny, then click on them, and post them on our website. We'd usually scroll through about a thousand new slogans a day on the website. Customers all over the world would order T-shirts. If nobody ordered a particular slogan, the website automatically dropped it off the list after a day. But if someone ordered a shirt with one of that day's slogans, then we'd keep that slogan on the website feed for that week. If more people bought it, we'd add it to our 'favorites' list. The website was designed to keep accumulating the most popular slogans and to dump ones that didn't sell."

"But, back to this app," Walt said. "How can an app write slogans that make any sense?"

"T-shirts don't have to make sense," Billy said. "People don't buy them because they make sense. In fact, sometimes, the stupider the slogan, the better."

Walt still looked confused, so Billy continued. "Look, I'd type in a word like 'slug' or 'lizard', and the app just generates slogans, like 'This Slug's for You' or 'Get Slug—Forget the Rest' or 'Lizard—Extra Dry' or 'I Feel like Lizard Tonight'. They're just t-shirt slogans, so they have to be short."

"Those don't make any sense, though," said Walt.

"They're impulse buys, like when you're standing in the checkout line and you grab a Snickers bar and add it to your grocery cart. Eating a candy bar doesn't make any sense either—they're bad for you and cost way too much. But it's an impulse. When these kids all over the world see a T-shirt online that appeals to them, they just have to make one click of a mouse to order it. That's less effort than reaching over and picking up a Snickers bar and dropping it in your cart. For example, one of our most popular lines are T-shirts that have the word 'risk' in them, like 'Risk Empowers You' and 'There's no Life Without Risk' and 'Just Risk'. We probably sell a thousand T-shirts a day to 10- and 11-year-old kids all over the world that have slogans with the word 'risk' in them— and these are kids who never leave their computers, never go outside."

"Really?" Walt asked. "That many? And they're all printed in our little town? I had no idea."

"Oh no," Billy sneered, "They're all printed and shipped out of China. It's all print-on-demand. Two minutes after some customer hits the 'Order' button and his credit card clears, that T-shirt is being printed, folded, packaged and shipped out of China."

"So…your office ran the website?"

"No," Billy said, "the server is in Costa Rica and the webmaster is somewhere in the Ukraine."

Both men sat silently for a moment, sipping at their beers. Finally Walt spoke:

"So, an app on a computer generates the slogans…and your job was to move the slogans from that computer onto a website that is based in Central America…and the customers order T-shirts from that website…and the website is designed to automatically select and offer the most popular slogans… and the website is managed from somewhere in the Ukraine… and the shirts are printed and shipped from China…"

"Yeah. Crazy, huh?" Billy said and took another sip of beer.

"Did your office handle the billing?"

"Nah, that was all done online. I think the credit card processing was outsourced to India," Billy said.

"And customer complaints?" Walt asked.

"Handled through a call center in Costa Rica," Billy replied. "No, once we generated the slogans, we were out of the loop. We never interacted with the customer, or saw the product, or anything."

"Wow," Walt said. "Well, excuse me for saying this, but there doesn't seem to be much need for this office."

"Yeah," Billy laughed, "Evidently they thought so too. That's why they let us all go. We got an email today saying they were closing the entire office, effective immediately. Some goons from a security firm showed up and we all had to leave the building."

"Wow, how many people worked there?"

"There were just three of us. Two slogan-guys and a manager."

"Wow," Walt said again. "So who's going to select their slogans now?"

"No one," Billy said. "Before the security dudes showed up, Mike—he was the boss—he made some frantic calls overseas. It turns out that they don't need anyone to select the slogans anymore. The programmers in the Ukraine came up with a new business model—they call it 'Natural Selection'. They programmed the website to generate random words and feed those random words into the app. Then, when the app generates slogans, the website just select slogans *at random* from the app and offers T-shirts with those slogans on them for sale on the website. It's a totally market-driven business now. If someone buys a slogan, it stays on the website. If no one buys it, it drops off the website. There's no human involvement in the process. They don't need slogan-guys anymore, because it doesn't matter if a slogan is totally illogical or stupid—it'll be gone by tomorrow. Over time, the market determines the most popular slogans. The company has grown so big now, that the sheer volume of business is selecting which slogans are funny based on which slogans get sold."

"Wow," Walt said and shook his head. "How big is this company?"

"They sell millions of T-shirts world-wide every day," Billy said. "Just millions."

"What is their name?"

"T-Shirts USA," Billy said.

"What's USA about them now?" Walt asked.

"The name," Billy said.

"Wow," Walt said. He looked over at Billy's empty glass. "Want another beer?"

Billy nodded his head. Walt raised two fingers to the barkeeper and pointed at him and Billy. The barkeeper nodded.

DEATH

Thomas was close to death. Or rather, he *felt* close to death. He didn't *know for a fact* that he was close to death. None of us know. That's why we go on, isn't it? I mean, when you really think about it, the only reason we go on is because we don't know when we are going to die, so we hope we will live forever, and so we do the things that people do when they think they're going to live forever: we go to school, start careers, get married, have affairs, get divorced—not necessarily all in that order. But the point is, we *go on* because we think our lives will *go on*. If we knew the hour of our death, well...why the fuck would we bother? There would be no point in going to school for three years if it was written that you were going to die in three months, would there? Think about it! If you knew you were going to die in three months, what would you do? Personally, I'd be thinking cocaine, whores, bathhouses, more whores...

But on the other hand, if you knew you were going to live to ninety, well then, investing a measly three years to get that graduate degree makes sense—because it would maximize your income, and when you compound that income over several decades, well... there's more money for that retirement cocaine, whores, bathhouses, more whores, etc. But I digress.

As I was saying, Thomas *felt* that death was close... nearby...in the vicinity. But he didn't *know*. All he had were clues: occasional minor chest pains, occasional weakness in his legs, occasional incontinence, forgetting things. But he had always had those. And he had always had them in the exact same amounts. It was just that now he noticed them more. His doctor just laughed and said Thomas was being a hypochondriac. Because the fact was, Thomas was in pretty good health, considering his age. He was sixty-seven. He had retired the year before, at sixty-six. He could have retired from his job at sixty-five, but he wanted that extra year of income while he waited for his Social Security payments to start. He could have taken Social Security early, as early as sixty-two, but then he would have received reduced payments, and he did not like the idea of reduced payments. Thomas always liked to maximize his investments. So he stayed with his job at the state for an extra year, maxing out his work pension, and he took Social Security at sixty-six to get the full payment. Plus, for the past fifteen years, he had also been taking advantage of his job's Deferred Compensation Program, taking only a portion of his salary, which helped reduce his taxes. By the time he retired last year, he had $600,000 in his Deferred Compensation Fund, which he rolled over—tax free—into his IRA at Undercroft Investments, LLC. Howard Wiser, his investment counselor at Undercroft, had been very helpful over the years in counseling Thomas on how to set up his retirement investments to get the maximum return. And thus, Thomas was able to retire with almost two million dollars in mix of stable, conservative, long-term mutual funds, index funds, stocks, bonds and cash reserves, plus two decent monthly checks—one from Social Security and one from his state pension plan. Thomas was as secure as one could be in his investments...but, as mentioned, not feeling as secure about his longevity.

He went back to see his doctor, Dr. Calvin Cho. Dr. Cho had been Thomas's physician for more than twenty years, and Thomas trusted him.

"Should I get another heart stress test?" Thomas asked after Dr. Cho listened to his heart.

"No," Dr. Cho said. "Your heart is fine. Besides, you just had a stress test this spring, and it was normal. We can do another one in maybe two years. Are you still jogging?"

"Yeah, but I don't seem to have the stamina that I used to," Thomas said.

"Well, Thomas, you're 67. Your body's going to be slowing down a little. How's your appetite?"

"It's good, but I don't seem to be enjoying food the way I used to."

"Uh huh. Well, look, maybe it's just the stress of retirement, Thomas. It's not easy, you know...making a major transition like retirement."

"Yeah," said Thomas.

The fact was, retirement had been pretty easy for Thomas. As was his nature, he had planned it out carefully, scheduling trips and activities to fill up his new free time. He had taken a budget vacation to Europe and hiked around Switzerland, staying in hostels. In fact, he was enjoying retirement immensely, except for that one thing: he was afraid that Time was going to swindle him out of his retirement savings.

His fear had all started about four months ago when he got a text message from Howard Wiser that only said, "Did you hear about Peter Corso?"

"No," Thomas texted back. "What about him?"

"He passed away."

Peter was the same age as Thomas and had retired a few months after Thomas had. Peter had worked with Howard at Undercroft. The three men would often have lunch together and talk about world politics and finances. Over the last year, much of the conversation had been around both Thomas's and Peter's retirement plans. Peter had bought a vacation home in Aruba and was looking forward to spending winters there with his wife.

"What?" Thomas had texted back when he read Howard's message.

But it was true. Peter had retired, spent one winter in Aruba, and had just returned home a month before he died. A sudden and unexpected heart attack took him out.

This news upset Thomas for months afterward. As mentioned, Peter was the same age, and had always appeared to Thomas to be in excellent health. Both men had similar ideas about life and the importance of financial planning, and they both shared a common excitement about their respective upcoming retirements. It just seemed so unfair to Thomas that death would take his friend just when he was about to enjoy the fruits of all his years of labor. He was only sixty-seven! He could have lived another twenty years, spending his winters in Aruba, sipping piña coladas on the beach, puttering in his garden at home during the summers, enjoying the grandkids.

And thus, when Thomas was in Howard's office recently, reviewing his portfolio, Peter's death was still on his mind.

"You know, Thomas," Howard was saying, "now that you're retired, you ought to start thinking about how to structure withdrawals from your retirement. We can set up monthly direct deposits into your checking account if you want."

"Well, to be honest, between my state pension and my Social Security payments, I have enough to live on," Thomas replied.

"True," Howard said, "but you could be enjoying a better standard of living. Remember when you complained about that economy flight to Europe? How the seats didn't recline so you couldn't sleep at all during the ten hour flight? You could have flown first class, where the seats recline all the way down."

"Well," Thomas laughed, "those first class seats cost five grand! Because I planned it out and bought my ticket in advance, I only paid nine hundred round trip!"

"Right...," Howard said slowly, "but why deny yourself that first class ticket now?' Howard paused, and then said, "Look, Thomas, I spend every hour of my professional day telling people to save, telling them to invest their money, to sock it away for a rainy day...but the whole point to that is to be able to spend that money at some point. I mean—and don't quote me on this—but it's only money. You don't have a wife or any kids. You've spent your whole life carefully investing. Why not spend a little now? What else are you going to do with that money?"

Howard looked at his computer screen. "You've got over two million dollars in investments. You could take out one hundred thousand a year for the next twenty years and add that your pension and Social Security money."

Thomas was quiet. As mentioned, the death of Peter was still weighing heavily on his mind. Finally, he said quietly, "Let me think on it a bit, Howard."

And it just so happened that the next day, Thomas got a call from Lois Albright, his insurance agent with State Allegiance Insurance.

"Hello Thomas," Lois said cheerfully. "How's retirement

treating you?"

"Pretty good, Lois. How are you?"

"Doing well, Thomas, thank you. You know, Thomas, I was just looking over your policies, and I was noticing a gap in your coverage."

"A gap?" Thomas said. He wasn't aware of any gap. He didn't own a home—he considered that a bad investment. He didn't need life insurance. He had Medicare Advantage and a supplement. So the only other insurance he needed was his automobile and his apartment rental insurance.

"What kind of gap?" he asked.

"Well, now that you're retired, you ought to consider long-term care insurance," Lois said.

"Why would I need that?" Thomas asked.

"Because it's the only way to protect your savings from the cost of nursing care. You know, Thomas, none of us like to think about getting older, but the fact is that seventy percent of us end up needing some type of nursing care at the end of our lives. And without long-term care insurance, that nursing care can completely deplete a lifetime of savings in just a few years. So maybe you'd like to come in and we could chat about this."

Thomas's initial reaction when Lois had used the phrase 'long-term care insurance' was negative. He certainly did not envision himself in a nursing home or needing any kind of live-in nurse, but the phrase "protect your savings" caught his ear, and so, being a careful and open-minded fellow, he agreed to go into Lois's office the next day and listen to her pitch.

The next day, as soon as he sat down, she started into her presentation:

"Did you know, Thomas," she asked, "that the average cost of a private room in a nursing home is over eighty-seven thousand a year?"

"Hmmm," Thomas said.

"And Medicare doesn't cover long-term care. And while it's unpleasant to think about, the reality is that seventy percent of people over the age of sixty-five will need some type of nursing care in their lives."

"Hmmm," Thomas said.

"The problem is, that long-term nursing care insurance isn't cheap. But the good news is that the sooner you sign up, the sooner you can lock your rates in. Once you sign up, your rates will never increase. And that's important because the cost of nursing care is going up, and the longer you live the better the odds are that you will need long-term nursing care."

"And how long is that?" Thomas asked.

"How long is what?"

"How long am I going to live?"

Lois looked at Thomas. "Well, ah, I certainly hope a long time, Thomas..."

"No, I'm serious, Lois. It just occurred to me while you were talking that insurance companies have the best aactuaries— the best statisticians for predicting how long people live, so that you know how to set the premium levels—otherwise insurance companies would go out of business—so you must have someone who can predict how long I'm going to live."

"Well, um, our policies are based on certain models, yes, that's true, and um, based on your age, your date of birth, whether you smoke, your medical history, this part of the country...yes, when we sign someone up, we have them fill out a questionnaire and we use that to calculate their premium, yes."

"Exactly," Thomas said. "That makes sense. You would take all those factors and you could calculate how long someone was going to live and probably, based on their medical and family history, the likelihood of whether they would need nursing care."

"Well...yes," Lois said.

"But *you* don't do that calculation, right?" Thomas asked.

"No, we send the questionnaire downtown. There's a specialist there who looks at it and sets the premium rate."

"Wonderful!" Thomas said. "I want to meet him."

"Well, Thomas, the formulas they use are based on proprietary information, industry secrets...even I don't know them..."

"No, no," explained Thomas. "I don't want to know *how* he does it. And I don't care what he thinks the odds are that I will need long-term nursing care or not. I just want him to give me the best scientific analysis of how long he thinks I will live. I'll fill out whatever questionnaire he wants, or undergo whatever medical test he wants me to take—hell, I'll even pay for any medical tests and his time in doing the math—I just want the best possible estimate of how much time I have."

Lois was taken back. "Well, Thomas, I—I don't know if I can arrange that."

Thomas leaned back in his chair and smiled. "Lois, I've been a policyholder with this company for 40 years. I like your insurance products. I keep the maximum coverage you offer on my car and my renter's insurance. I have my Medicare Advantage policy through you. I'm a long-term customer. But this policy you're offering me now is quite different from my other policies. How can I reasonably evaluate whether I should sign up for this insurance without knowing how long I am going to live? It's a reasonable request. See what you can do."

Two weeks later, Thomas was sitting back in Howard Wiser's office.

"So I met with this kid," Thomas was explaining. "He was their statistician. Nice kid, bright as shit, but young. Anyway, I filled out a long questionnaire, met with their doctor, had some blood tests, and some x-rays..."

"They do this with all their clients?" Howard asked.

"No, no, I asked as a special favor, and it turned out they were wanting to test some of their statistical models, so it kind of worked out that they agreed to this. Anyway, they talked with my doctor and got my health history, and they did all these tests and stuff, and then they fed all this data into their computer—and they've got these sophisticated algorithms and decades of data about people's longevity, their lifestyles and health, and all that stuff, and they compared me to millions of other people with the same genetic background and same health habits—and they said that, statistically, they estimated I would die at age 74."

"They said that?" Howard asked, amazed.

"Well, they phrased it nicely, Howard. They said there was a ninety percent chance I'd live to age 70; an eighty-three percent chance I'd live to 73; and a nine percent chance I'd live to 75. You don't have to be a math scientist to see what that means."

"That's horrible!" Howard said. "I can't believe they said that! In fact, I don't believe it! That's only 7 years from now."

"I know," said Thomas.

"That's just horrible," Howard said again.

"No it's not," Thomas said. "Actually, it's great news."

"What?"

"Well, remember you and I talked a few weeks back about my taking a monthly disbursement from my investment fund?" Thomas asked.

"Yeah."

"Well, truth be told, Howard, I couldn't do it. I mean, at that time I couldn't do it. I was afraid that if I took too much out, I would end up alone and broke, but that if I didn't take enough out, I would die while there was still tons of money left in the fund. I was paralyzed because I didn't have any basis—any data—on which to make a rational decision of how much to take. But now I know. Now I have a scientific method for deciding how much money to take out of the fund every year."

Howard stared at Thomas. He thought about it for a minute, and then said, "Well you know, that...kind of... makes sense, Thomas."

"Yes, it does. I grilled this kid, Howard. I asked him point blank if he was saying I was going to die at seventy-four. And then I grilled him on his degree of certainty. This kid is an M.I.T. graduate. Not only did he have a 93.5% degree of certainty about my dying at age seventy-four, but he narrowed it down to the month....November, give or take ten days."

"That's amazing!" Howard said.

"Yup, I know," Thomas said, and smiled.

"So...what are your thoughts about the disbursement?" Howard asked.

Thomas pulled a piece of paper out of his pocket. "I've done some calculations, Howard. It doesn't make sense to take the same amount out each year, because the older I get, the more expensive things will become, so I've worked out a progression. I'm going to start off with smaller amount, and then increase it every year. So this year, I want to withdraw one hundred fifty grand...so that's twelve thousand five hundred a month. Next year, I want to withdraw two hundred grand; the third year I want to withdraw two hundred fifty grand, etc., etc. Here's the progression." And Thomas handed the chart to Howard.

Howard studied it for a moment, and then said, "We can do this. No problem, Thomas, we can make this work for you."

"Oh, Howard, it's going to be great. I'm going to travel, but I'm going to do it first class. I want to go back to Europe this year, and I still want to hike, maybe the Camino de Santiago trail in Spain. But no more hostels for me—just first class lodging all the way. And first class airfare, too. This is going to be so great! Next year, I plan to go to Australia and New Zealand. I figure that by the fifth and sixth year, I'll start slowing down, be doing less hiking, and will stay with just ocean cruises and river cruises. There are some great river cruises in Europe. But I'm going to enjoy myself. I'm going to have fun!"

"I am so excited for you, Thomas," Howard said. "You know, this is the part of my job that I love the best. When people finally retire and can really enjoy what they've worked so hard to achieve. I tell you what: leave this chart with me, and I'll draw up all the legal disbursement papers, and tell the home office what we're doing, and...can you come back this afternoon around two? I should have everything all printed out by then. We can sign all the documents and set up automatic deposits into your checking account, starting... what? On the first of each month?"

"First of each month sounds good to me, Howard. I'm going to go grab a bite to eat, and then go home for a bit and get online and look at airplane schedules, and I'll be back here at two."

"Sounds great, Thomas," Howard said, standing up. Both men shook hands and Thomas left the building.

Thomas was feeling good, better than he had been in months. He was smiling and thinking about where he was going to have lunch. He was going to have fun. He was going to start living now. People would ask, "How's Thomas doing?" And someone would say, "He's living the dream."

Thomas never saw the truck that rounded the corner as he stepped off the curb. The coroner said that he probably never felt a thing, as the initial impact would have knocked him cold, and that the tremendous weight of the truck's wheels crushed his ribcage and stopped his heart immediatcly.

TOP TEN SCIENCE FACTS NOT TAUGHT IN SCHOOL

1. The purpose of flatulence is to push the poop out of your body. That's how evolution has designed your digestion system. Your body creates just enough gas to propel your poop out when you sit on a toilet. Every time you fart, you are wasting gas and increasing the odds that you will be constipated. You should always hold your farts in until you can poop.

2. "There is someone for everyone," they say. But it's not true. Statistically speaking, only 9% of people find someone. Everyone else is lying.

3. Speaking of lying, it is a statistical fact that every word someone says is a lie. 100% of the time.

4. A recent survey of U.S. Congressmen (just the men) revealed that 63% of them do not know how babies are born. The other 37% know, but don't care.

5. There are 10 secrets for a perfect life. You will never discover them.

6. Sex is better with someone else. However, it's much, much better with two other people. Always buy a bed big enough for three people.

7. There are many gods, and most of them hate us.

8. Mankind did alright until writing was invented. As soon as there was writing, there were laws. It's been all downhill since then.

9. Everything is political, whether it's one other person, or a small office, or Congress. Every single interaction is political. And politics is about control. And by "control" I mean "enslavement", i.e., they want to enslave you. Whether you train a dog with treats or with a whip, it's still enslavement. People want to enslave you, whether it's one other person, or a small office, or Congress. Why? Because people are no damn good.

10. The only thing that matters is what matters to you. Everything else is distraction.

THE BAD LUCK CLUB

Johnny Hasenfus always had the worst luck. It seemed he was born with bad luck. His dad had a successful farm south of Chillicothe, but then, when Johnny was seven, his dad suffered a freak accident with a chainsaw and died. His mother tried to keep the farm going, but she didn't really know what she was doing, and the bank took the farm when Johnny was nine. He went to live with his aunt and uncle in Hillsboro, but something happened with his uncle that Johnny never talks about. The uncle went to prison, and Johnny ended up being passed around to a series of relatives. He failed most of his classes in school. It wasn't that he was stupid. He just couldn't focus. But the schools kept promoting him anyway. During the summers he worked as a pinsetter in different bowling alleys and dreamed of owning his own bowling business. But then, bowling went out of style, and bowling alleys all over the country started to close. At eighteen, he got a job in a print shop, setting linotype. He liked doing that, and dreamed of owning his own typesetting shop one day. But computer printers put an end to that dream. At twenty, he moved to Detroit, and got a job in a Ford assembly factory. He took that job because it had a secure future, but then the factory closed down. He decided to try something different, so he moved to Houston and got a low-level job at a company called Enron. When Enron collapsed, he moved to Mississippi and got a job at MCI WorldCom, Inc., but then their founder Bernie Ebbers went to jail, and that company—and his job—disappeared. After that, he got a job at K-Mart. After K-Mart filed for bankruptcy, Johnny got a job with Adelphia Communications, and then Circuit City. Both went bankrupt.

Johnny's friends would always tell him that it was just bad luck, but Johnny's resume looked like a Who's Who of American frauds, fuck-ups, disasters, and failures. After a while, he simply started omitting some of the more infamous places he had worked: Enron, Tyco, HealthSouth, WorldCom, and Waste Management.

But Johnny thought that maybe his bad luck with jobs was simply a result of his lack of education. He enrolled in ITT Technical College after a recruiter told him that a good education would change his life. It was on a bulletin board in the lunchroom at ITT that Johnny saw the 3x5 card about the Bad Luck Club.

The 3x5 card was old with bent edges, but the title caught Johnny's eye:

> *Are you plagued by misfortune?*
> *Join the Bad Luck Club*
> *And change your luck.*

At the bottom was a telephone number. Johnny didn't think he would ever need such a group, now that he was going to get an education and change his life. But on a whim, he jotted the number down in a little notebook of positive affirmations he kept in his front shirt-pocket.

A few days later, Johnny and the rest of the students arrived at the school to find the doors locked and a sign posted on the door that said, "It is with profound regret that we must report that ITT Educational Services, Inc., will discontinue all academic services immediately." Johnny went back to his apartment and called the number of the Bad Luck Club. He got a recorded message that simply said that the club met every Wednesday in the basement room of a local Unitarian Church, and that membership was free.

The next day was Wednesday. Since Johnny no longer had to spend his evenings doing homework, he had nothing else to do, so he decided to go to the meeting. He figured he would just observe and see what it was about.

The Unitarian Church was close enough to his apartment so that he could walk there. He entered the main door, found a placard in the hall that informed him which stairway to take to the meeting of the Bad Luck Club, and he walked down the stairs and into a big room. A group of people were seated in a big circle of folding metal chairs in the center of the room. There was a side table with a Mr. Coffee and Styrofoam cups. Johnny normally didn't drink coffee at night because it kept him up. But since he saw that everyone else in the circle was holding a cup of coffee, he figured he would get one so he would look like he fit in. He poured himself a cup of coffee— it smelt horrible—and he walked over to the circle and sat in one of the empty seats. Some people nodded or smiled at him, but no one said anything. He just sat there, sipping at the horrible coffee, and waited for whatever was going to happen next.

After about five minutes, an older gaunt-looking man spoke up.

"Well, I guess we might as well get started. I see we have several new faces here tonight, so I'll explain how this group works. This is a self-help group for people with bad luck. We meet here every Wednesday night, but we're not affiliated with the church. There is a small donation box on the table next to the coffeepot where people can make a donation to the church as a way of thanking them for letting us use their space and to help them defray the cost of the coffee, but that donation is voluntary. There are no fees associated with this group. It is totally free. You might consider that, in itself, as a stroke of good luck.

"My name is Todd, and I am the group leader. My job is simply to encourage people to talk, nothing more. As I mentioned, we are a self-help group. The only structure is that we go around, one-by-one, introduce ourselves—first names only—and say a few words about our lives. We're all here for the same reason: We all have rotten luck. The theory behind this group is that somehow, in sharing our bad luck stories with others, that a healing process might occur, both for ourselves and for the others in the group. So, who would like to start?"

A very plain looking woman sitting across the circle from Johnny raised her hand. Todd nodded at her and said, "Okay, Nancy, thank you."

"My name is Nancy," the woman said, "and I would say that this week was one of the worst weeks I've had in a long while. First, my car got hit in the Walmart parking lot. I had gone there to buy cat litter, and when I came out, there was a huge dent on the driver's side of my car. Someone had just backed into it, and then taken off. I couldn't even get the door open. I had to climb into my car through the passenger door, and climb over the stick shift to get to the driver's seat. I called my insurance company and they told me a body shop to take the car to, so I took it there, and they estimated the repair would be two hundred dollars. But my deductible is two hundred, and I don't have that kind of money. So now, every time I want drive my car, I have to get in and out through the passenger side. Plus, my insurance company told me they have to raise my rates, because this is my third accident this year. I complained that it wasn't my fault, just like the other two accidents weren't my fault, but they said that was their policy, and it was just my bad luck."

Todd nodded his head sympathetically and said, "That certainly is unfortunate, Nancy. I'm sure I speak for everyone in saying that that was really bad luck. Thank you for sharing. Who else would like to introduce themselves?"

A rather obese man spoke up. "My name is Gerald. Last week I was in one of those health food stores, and the clerk convinced me to try these seeds—they were like small pods—from some tree—I forget the name. Anyway, he told me it was a natural organic appetite suppressant—that I would lose weight because I wouldn't be hungry. So I bought a bunch. And I did lose a little weight at first, because it made me throw up all night, but then the next morning I was starving so I ate a huge breakfast. I tried it one more time, but it turned my skin all splotchy and I had to stay inside for a day, and I don't have any sick days left, so I lost out on a day of pay, plus I paid thirty-five dollars for these seeds that don't work. So I threw them away."

Todd nodded and said, "Thank you Gerald."

Another man spoke up. "My name is Tim. My unemployment ran out last week. I've been using the library's computer to apply for jobs, but the library is closed this week because they're investigating that man who overdosed and died in the men's room. So I have to wait another week before I can apply for a job."

A woman spoke up. "My name is Ilene. I work as a waitress at IHOP and the other day a man left me a huge tip when he paid by credit card, and I was excited because I was going to get some extra money, but then right after the customer left, the bank called and said that the credit card was stolen. And IHOP has this policy that if a customer doesn't pay for a meal for any reason, the cost of the meal comes out of the waitress' salary, so I had to pay for his breakfast. But then they made me pay for the tip too! And I never got the tip. The manager said that their policy was that the waitress had to repay the entire bill and he interpreted that to mean including the tip, even if IHOP never gave me the tip money."

Another man spoke up. "My name is James, and my divorce was finalized last week, and my wife got custody of our son. Only, it turns out that he's not my son. She'd been having an affair for the last four years with some guy while I was at work, and the child is his. But she told me I was the father and I believed her. But my lawyer had some DNA tests done, and he's not my son. But the court says that I have to pay the child support because I didn't contest paternity in time. Well, I didn't know! My lawyer says I'm stuck paying child support until the boy is eighteen because that's the law."

Everyone in the circle told their story. Finally, Todd looked at Johnny. Johnny didn't know what to say, but he spoke. "Um, my name is Johnny, and I was going to ITT, but it closed yesterday, but I still have all these student loans to pay." He couldn't think of anything else to say, so he just looked at Todd and shrugged his shoulders.

Todd said, "Thank you for sharing, Johnny, and welcome to our group."

Johnny went home that night and thought about his experience with the group. He didn't feel particularly better having listened to everyone else's story, but he didn't feel worse, either. He recognized that his situation was not as bad as some of the people in the group. He decided to go back the following week. Maybe over time, he thought, going to the group might help him.

And so each week Johnny went back to the group, and sat there holding a styrofoam cup of coffee and listening to everyone speak. And Johnny spoke too, although his stories were often short. "I'm still looking for work," or "The student loan people called me again this week—they want me to start making payments," or "I had an interview but didn't get the job."

He kept going back each week for the same reason he went the first night. He simply didn't have anything better to do. It didn't seem to help, but it didn't seem to hurt either, so he kept going back.

Finally, Johnny got a job working at a local circular called *Penny Saved*. It was a four-page weekly newsletter that was distributed free to laundromats or pizza joints or doctors' waiting rooms. It had handy tips on gardening, a section for jokes and riddles, and two pages of ads for swap-meets, for-sale items, announcements, garage sales, etc. Johnny's job was to deliver bundles of the current edition to all the locations and pick up the old copies of last week's edition. It was a stupid job, but he didn't qualify for unemployment because his enrollment in ITT had broken the chain of his periods of employment that would have entitled him to unemployment benefits.

But it was in the classified ads in the back of *Penny Saved* that Johnny saw the ad for Madam Lin, Fortune Teller. Johnny had actually heard of her before. Madam Lin was a well-known Chinese palm-reader in the community. The ad in Penny Saved was a coupon for half-off a palm reading. Johnny decided that maybe a professional opinion by Madam Lin might be helpful. Maybe she could give him some guidance on how to change his luck. So he called and made an appointment.

Johnny pressed the buzzer on the door and waited. A young Chinese girl came to the door and opened it an inch.

"I have an appointment," Johnny said hopefully.

The girl nodded and let him in. Then she locked the door behind her.

"You can't be too safe," Johnny offered, hoping to break the ice, but she ignored his comment and silently pointed to a beaded doorway.

Johnny parted the beads with his hands and stepped inside the darkened room. Madam Lin was sitting at a small table. Johnny smiled hopefully and sat down in the chair across from her.

She looked at him, at his face. He started to hold out his palms for her to look at, but she just shook her head no, and continued to look at his face.

Finally she spoke. "I can see your problem. You have a low hairline. In China, we have a saying: 'People with low hairlines have bad luck.' Your problem is you have bad luck. It's because you have a low hairline. There is nothing I can do."

Johnny looked at her and waited, but after another minute it was clear she wasn't going to say anything more.

"Is there something I can do?" he started to ask.

"There is nothing more I can tell you," she said. "You go now."

"But..." he started to protest.

"You go now," she repeated.

"Okay," Johnny said, and stood up. "How much do I owe you?"

"Nothing. You go now. You have low hairline. There is nothing I can do. You have bad luck. So sorry."

Johnny left Madam Lin's storefront business and went home. He felt very confused. When he got back to his apartment, he went into the bathroom and looked at the mirror. He *did* have a very low hairline. It ran straight across his forehead. He only had about an inch and a half of forehead between the top of his eyebrows and where his hairline began. Johnny went into his living room, sat down on the couch, and began to think. Maybe this was his problem. Maybe it wasn't bad luck so much as some type of genetic curse. Maybe a low hairline was a marker, like wearing a "kick me" sign, so that when he stepped out of his apartment in the morning, the gods knew who to fuck with. Maybe if he changed his appearance, his luck would change. He went and got a pair of tweezers from the bathroom cabinet and stood in front of the mirror and started plucking hairs out of his forehead. One by one, he yanked the hairs out, and gradually, over the course of the next hour, he reshaped his hairline, moving it up almost two inches higher. He changed the shape as well, creating a nice curve that went back further on the sides. The sink was full of hairs.

After an hour, he put the tweezers down and examined his new face. He liked it. It didn't look like him at all. He moved his head left and right and up and down. The image in the mirror was of a stronger, more confident man. Johnny liked what he saw.

He looked at his watch. It was almost six and he was hungry. He decided to go down to Molly's Grill and get dinner.

Luckily, Molly's wasn't crowded. He sat at the bar and ordered fajitas and a beer. He waited for his dinner and sipped his beer. There was large mirror behind the bar, and Johnny looked at his reflection and wondered if his new hairline would make any difference.

In the reflection he saw a young woman enter the bar. She was very pretty, tall and blond. She looked at the empty booths, but then took a seat several bar stools away from Johnny. She picked up one of the menus and started to look through it. Johnny assumed she was waiting for someone to meet her, probably her husband or a date. He had long since stopped talking to women in bars, or anywhere else for that matter.

The waitress brought Johnny's fajitas to him, and he started to eat.

"That looks good," he heard the woman say. He looked over. She was talking to him. "What is it?" she asked.

Johnny wiped his mouth with his napkin and said, "They're fajitas. They're very good here."

"What's in them?" she asked.

"Just strips of beef, grilled onions, green peppers, and tomatoes. It's a simple recipe. But the secret here is that they marinate the beef."

"Oooh, I'm going to try those," the lady said and signaled to the waitress.

Johnny continued to eat his fajitas and sip at his beer. What an odd thing, he thought—for a woman to talk to him. But the woman didn't say anything more, so he shrugged it off.

The waitress brought a plate of fajitas and a glass of wine to the woman.

"Oh my God," the woman exclaimed to Johnny when she took her first bite, "These are wonderful!"

"Yeah, I always order them here," Johnny said. "This place is known for them...at least in this town, anyway."

"Are you from here?" the woman asked.

"No, no I'm from Ohio originally," Johnny said.

"No kidding!" the woman said, "I'm from Fairborn, Ohio. Where in Ohio are you from?"

"Chillicothe," Johnny said, then added, "I've been to Fairborn—that's a nice little town."

"Yes it is," the woman said. "I like little towns so much better than big cities."

"Me too," Johnny said, with just a touch of sadness.

"What brought you here?" the woman asked.

"Oh it's a long story," Johnny said. "I had enrolled at ITT Technical college. I was wanting to learn computer programming. But evidently the federal government closed them down. I don't know all the details, except that now I'm on the hook for all these student loans for a school that no longer exists, for classes that never started."

"Really!" the woman exclaimed. "Well, this is your lucky day! I work for the Federal Department of Education. They sent me here to get in touch with all the students from ITT and to arrange for loan forgiveness for them. I just arrived here in town about an hour ago, and I'm supposed to go over to the ITT building tomorrow and start looking through all their files."

Johnny couldn't believe his ears. "Really?" he said. "You're not joking?"

"No, really. My name's Emily." She stood up and brought her plate over to the seat next to Johnny and sat down and extended her hand. Johnny shook it and said, "My name's Johnny."

"Well, Johnny, I feel so lucky I came into this restaurant tonight. I tell you what—If you'll show me where the school is tomorrow, I'll make sure I process your loan forgiveness first. There are some forms to fill out and stuff, but we have this new program that will wipe out that ITT debt and also clear up any credit problems you have on your credit history because of ITT."

"Really? Sure, I'd be glad to show you the school and also around town tomorrow."

Johnny and Emily talked together for another hour that evening. He walked her back to her hotel and they made plans to meet the next morning so that he could show her the ITT campus.

When Wednesday night rolled around, it was a different Johnny Hasenfus that walked into the Bad Luck Club. Todd noticed it right away and addressed him at the beginning of the session.

"Johnny, you look different this week. I can't quite put my finger on it, but you look different. How was your week?"

"It was good. I met someone and...well, I guess we're dating...and she helped me get my student loan dismissed."

Gerald piped up from across the room. "You're dating? Did anything bad happen during the date?"

"No…not that I can think of," Johnny said. "We've gone out three times now, and they've all been good dates. I really like this woman."

Nancy asked him, "And that ITT student loan is gone?"

"Yeah," Johnny said.

"No bad luck at all this week?" Nancy asked incredulously.

"No…I guess not," Johnny said.

"Wow," Nancy said.

A murmur went through the group. This had never happened before.

"Well, this is refreshing," Todd finally said. "Maybe coming here helped."

Johnny just nodded his head and thought about Madam Lin. He was going to say something about how he had altered his hairline, but he looked around the room. Gerald's hairline wasn't low. Neither was Todd's. There was no consistent pattern to the hairlines of the people in the group. Maybe bad luck came for a variety of reasons or from different sources—like different curses—and his source happened to be his hairline. He just didn't know. But he decided not to share his experience with Madam Lin with the group because he thought they would think he was crazy.

The following week he noticed the hairs trying to grow back on his forehead, so he carefully plucked them out again with the tweezers. He even reshaped his hairline and moved it higher by about a millimeter. He thought that made him look better. He bought a new suit. He bought new shoes. He started getting job interviews.

At the next Wednesday meeting of the Bad Luck Club, he decided to play it low key. After all, things seemed to be going okay for him and he didn't want to jinx it. Emily and he were spending more time together. He had gotten invited back for a second interview on two jobs. He had joined a gym and had started working out. When he listened to everyone else in the group summarize their week, he realized he had had a damn good week.

"And how was your week," Todd finally asked him.

"It was alright," Johnny just said.

He noticed Gerald frowning at him. "Nothing bad happened?" Gerald asked.

"Nothing horrible," Johnny said.

Gerald continued to frown.

The following week, Johnny got hired at a new job working in a customer service center for an internet travel company. His job was simple: If people had a problem with the hotel or cruise or tour package that they had booked through the travel company, they would call the customer service center and he would try and help them resolve the problem. Johnny did well at the job because he had two qualities that his bosses liked: he was patient and he was used to things going wrong. This, of course, he had learned from his many years of bad luck. But the customers on the other end of the phone seemed to appreciate that he listened to them and was genuinely sympathetic. The other workers in the call center were always rushed to "solve the customer's problem" but Johnny always took the time to ask the customers "how they felt" about their misfortune—and that always seemed to calm them down. Then he would put them on hold and call the hotel or the tour provider and try and resolve the problem. He quickly learned that resolving the problem was never difficult because the hotel or service provider didn't want the travel company to stop sending them customers. But the customers thought it was Johnny's magic touch that made the difference—so he got good feedback from his customers and his bosses noted that.

He and Emily continued dating. That seemed to be going well. They seemed to fit together nicely, and he felt lucky to have met her. They started talking about possibly living together.

Johnny continued to monitor his hairline daily, plucking out any tiny hairs that wanted to grow back, and sometimes reshaping his hairline and moving it even higher on his forehead.

He went back to the Bad Luck Club a few more times, but started to feel ostracized by the members. His luck had changed, and he no longer fit in, so he stopped going.

After a few weeks, he got a promotion at work, and was put in charge of training new call center employees. He would sit them in a circle, just like the Bad Luck Club meetings, and have them each share horrible things that had happened to them in their lives. He never commented or preached to them, or even tried to teach them anything about customer service. The only format of these meetings was to talk about misfortune. But it seemed to work. The new hires came away from those meetings with a newfound ability to sympathize with the other people in the group, and that seemed to transfer over to their phone skills. His bosses were very impressed by Johnny's skill at training new employees. They sent a recommendation to their regional manager about promoting him to Director of Training for the whole region. The regional manager came and observed Johnny's groups and was impressed.

One day, out of the blue, Emily asked him, "Was your father bald?"

"No, no he wasn't," Johnny said. "Why?"

"Well, you have a receding hairline. I've noticed it over the past few months, and I was just wondering if you were going bald."

This bothered Johnny. He really liked Emily and didn't want to do anything to displease her. So he stopped moving his hairline back each morning, although he still would pluck out any tiny new hairs that were growing on his forehead.

The following week, however, he got rear-ended in traffic.

He was just sitting at a red light, and someone plowed into his car from behind. He wasn't hurt, but the impact bent his car frame and the car repair place quoted him five thousand to repair it. Unfortunately, the driver of the other car didn't have any insurance, and Johnny's own insurance had a high deductible.

"Bad luck," Emily said, trying to be helpful. He had never told her about his history of bad luck or his experience at the Bad Luck Club, so he just said, "Yeah." But inside, he was worried.

That same week, his bosses came to him and said that while the regional manager had been very impressed by his skills, budget restraints made it impossible to promote him this year. Johnny just nodded his head and said he understood. When he got home to his apartment, there was an email from his insurance company that said that they had decided to "total" the car—that the cost of repair exceeded the Blue Book value of the car, which they estimated to be three thousand. The letter said that he would receive a check for that amount in the next few weeks. Johnny dug out his most recent car payment bill and looked up how much he still owed on the car. He still owed four thousand two hundred fifty-three dollars. Johnny went into the bathroom with the tweezers and plucked out enough hairs to move his hairline up a full millimeter.

Because he had no car, Johnny had been taking the bus to work. He left his apartment early the next morning and walked to the bus stop and checked the bus schedule that was posted inside the bus shelter. Luckily, the next bus would be there in five minutes. Because he had a few minutes to wait, he went into a nearby 7-11 and bought a cup of coffee to go and a scratch-off lottery ticket. He stuck the lottery ticket in his pocket and went back outside just in time to catch his bus.

He forgot about the lottery ticket until he got to his desk at work. He fished it out of his pocket and scratched off the silver foil. He had won twenty thousand dollars. He couldn't believe it. He could pay off his car loan and be able to buy a nice new small car. He called Emily to tell her the good news.

"Wow," she said. "You really have good luck!"

"Well," Johnny replied, "the best luck I've ever had was meeting you."

"Awww, you're so sweet." There was a pause on the line, then she said, "You know, Johnny, I think I love you."

"I think I love you too, Emily."

That was the first time either one of them had said the L word to each other. Emily promised to make him a special dinner that night at her apartment. Johnny spent the rest of the day walking around on cloud nine. He felt like he was the luckiest guy in the whole wide world.

And so it went for Johnny for the next six months. He continued to pluck the hairs out of his forehead and reshape his hairline. Slowly his hairline moved back, higher and higher up his head. But the plucking was taking more and more of his time, almost two hours every day. He found an electrology clinic in his neighborhood. The lady who did the electrolysis asked Johnny if he understood that this was a permanent hair removal process. He said he understood. He started going once a week. The lady removed all the hairs that he used to spend hours plucking, and slowly they began reshaping his hairline, moving it higher and higher, a millimeter at a time. Johnny asked Emily if she cared that he was losing his hair, and she reassured him no, that she would love him forever. He took to wearing stylish caps whenever he went out—jaunty fedoras or colorful skull caps depending on his mood.

And his good luck continued. His employers found enough budget money to promote him to Director of Training for the whole region. He got to travel to different areas and give training sessions. Emily would go with him whenever she could get time away from work. They took some vacations together. One time they went to Vegas and Johnny hit a huge jackpot at the slot machines. He invested the money in stocks and they started doing really well. He and Emily started talking about getting married.

*   *   *

A year later, on a Wednesday night, Johnny walked back into the Bad Luck Club wearing a bright red skull cap. It took Todd a minute to recognize him.

"Johnny!" Todd said. "I didn't recognize you. Come on in. Grab some coffee and have a seat."

Johnny got a cup of coffee from the side table and looked around the room. There were a few new members, but he recognized all the old ones: Gerald, Nancy, Tim, Ilene, James, and the rest.

"How have you been?" Todd asked.

"Not so good, Todd...not so good," Johnny said.

"What happened?" asked Todd.

"I lost my job recently, and my girlfriend left me for another man."

"Oh no, I'm really sorry to hear that," Todd said.

"Yeah," Johnny said, and he removed his hat. Nancy and a few others gasped. He was completely bald.

"What happened to your hair?" Nancy asked.

Johnny shrugged and just said, "I went bald."

The group stared at his totally hairless, shiny head.

"Will it grow back?" Nancy asked.

"No," Johnny said sadly. It's all gone...gone permanently. And when there was no more hair, that's when things started to change. Everything fell apart. I had invested all my money in a stock brokerage house that turned out to be just a huge pyramid scheme, and I lost it all. The tour company I was working for decided to outsource all their customer service work to India and so everyone here was let go. My new car got repossessed. I was supposed to get married, but like I said, she dumped me for some other guy. Plus, I just found out this week that my apartment building has been sold, and all of us tenants have to be out by the first of the month.

"Wow," Gerald said sincerely. "That really is bad luck."

People around the group nodded.

Finally Todd said, "Well, damn...welcome back, Johnny."

AN INCREDIBLE LIGHTNESS OF BEING

Jannette woke up weightless. Only the weight of the sheet and the light blanket kept her from floating up to the ceiling.

"Well, this is odd," she thought. It wasn't an unpleasant feeling, being weightless, but it definitely wasn't normal. She floated there for a moment and thought about it. "I guess I'd better go see my doctor," she said out loud to the empty room.

Getting out of bed wasn't difficult. She used the bedposts to propel herself over toward her bathroom. But she discovered that using the bathroom was very challenging. Not only was she weightless, but her pee was also weightless. As she sat on the toilet and peed, it simply ran up in between her legs and up into the air in front of her and hovered there in tiny droplets... or it snuck around her ass and up her sides. She propped her feet up on the toilet seat, holding onto it with both hands, and aimed her pee as best she could towards the front of the bowl so the pee would rise in front. After she finished peeing, she just sat there and watched the liquid bubbles of pee floating there in front of her. She noticed they seemed to be attracted to each other. The small drops would merge with other drops and then with larger globules until, after a few minutes, there was just one large pulsating bubble in front of her.

Jannette frowned. She had heard of people becoming weightless before, but no one had ever said anything about pee being weightless. How was she supposed to manage that?

She found a ziploc bag in the drawer of her vanity, emptied all the Q-tips out of it, and captured the floating pee by carefully sliding the open bag down around the large pee bubble. She sealed the bag and released it. It gently floated downward, hovering inches above the ground. The weight of the bag did not quite cancel out the weightlessness of the pee. It looked like a Portuguese man-o-war drifting across the bottom of the ocean, a large clear envelope holding a slightly yellow liquid rising up from the floor, floating low because of the weight of the plastic ziploc slider bag.

"I wonder if the weightlessness of the pee goes away over time," she thought to herself. "Or does it always stay weightless?"

She propelled herself back into her bedroom and found her cell phone and called her doctor's office. Because she was dialing, she couldn't hold onto anything, so she just floated in the middle of the room. The doctor's receptionist answered. Jannette remembered her. She was an older lady who was a bit cranky. Her name was "Miss Amul" on the nameplate at the reception desk, with the emphasis on "Miss." Jannette explained that she was a patient of Dr. Benson's and needed to see him today.

"The doctor doesn't have any appointments available until next week," Miss Amul replied, "unless this is an emergency."

"Well, I need to see him today," Jannette said. "I woke up weightless, and I think that counts as an emergency."

Miss Amul paused, then said, "Let me put you on hold."

Jannette waited patiently. Bad music played on the phone—something by Barry Manilow. Jannette assumed that Miss Amul had selected the music.

Miss Amul came back on the line. "The doctor can see you in one hour," she said curtly.

"Thank you," Jannette said. "I'll be there."

Jannette hung up the phone and propelled herself into the kitchen. She had just enough time to eat something and take a shower. She grabbed a banana and a bran muffin and poured herself a glass of orange juice. She had prepared the coffee pot the night before so all she had to do was hit the start button on the coffee maker.

While the coffee was brewing, she sat at the kitchen table, wrapping her feet around the legs of the chair to hold herself down, and ate her muffin and banana. "Maybe this is just something that is going around, like a cold," she thought. "Maybe the doctor will give me a shot and tell me to spend the rest of the day in bed and that I'll be fine tomorrow." Jannette hoped that would be the case. She figured she could manage peeing at home, but that managing weightless pee in public restrooms would be very difficult. The coffee maker buzzed, and she poured herself a cup of coffee. She re-anchored herself to the chair, drank her coffee and tried to remember everything she had ever read about people who born weightless, or who woke up weightless, or who became weightless. The problem was that she had never thought it would happen to her, so she hadn't paid much attention to the many articles she had seen. She realized that she would have to ask her doctor a lot of questions.

But now it was time to shower. She propelled herself back towards the bathroom. Halfway there, she realized she had to poop. "Shit!" she said out loud and began to panic. It was one thing to deal with floating pee, but dealing with floating poop would be horrible. How was she going to handle this?

But the thing about poop is: poop doesn't wait for you to figure things out. Jannette had to poop and that was it. "Damn bran muffins and coffee," she said, as she held herself down on the toilet by grasping both sides of the toilet seat. She closed her eyes and let herself poop and prepared for the worst.

But the worst didn't happen. The poop just fell out and landed in the toilet water, like it always did. Jannette breathed a big sigh of relief. "Thank God," she said aloud.

Jannette finished pooping and then took a shower. After drying herself, she propelled herself to her bedroom closet and started picking out what to wear. As she tried on different outfits, she realized that heavier clothes made it easier to move around. She put on a pair of jeans and a belt that had a large metal buckle, and a bra, t-shirt and blouse. Once she had some jewelry on and had put her shoes on, she no longer had to propel herself from object to object in order to move—she could just walk like normal...well, almost normal. She could cover a lot of ground with a single step. But with a few minutes of practice, she saw how she could appear as if she were walking normally by just taking what felt like tiny steps. "That's good," she thought to herself. "I don't want to stand out from the crowd."

Driving wasn't that difficult, either. Jannette's seatbelt kept her anchored to the seat and her shoes kept her feet down near the pedals. "I'm starting to get the hang of this," she thought.

"The reason your stool doesn't float," the doctor explained, "is that it's not part of you—it's just undigested food. Your body has absorbed all the nutrients out of the food, and defecating is just your body's way of getting rid of the food material that remains. Urine, on the other hand, is part of you—it's liquid that your body has created to flush out waste chemicals, so it floats...just like you do."

"How long will the pee float?" Jannette asked, "And for that matter, how long will I float?"

"That depends," Dr. Benson said, "on why you are floating,

or rather…which of the two floating viruses you have caught. Right now, there are two floating viruses that we're dealing with in this hemisphere. One, called HTZ6, is permanent. Once you get it, you will be weightless for the rest of your life. Luckily, most insurance covers the classes and physical therapy you would need to take to adjust to your new state of being. But HTZ6 is pretty rare. The second type, called HQU3, is actually more common, and it only lasts 12 to 15 hours. When you wake up tomorrow, you will know which type you have. If you have your weight back, that means you had HQU3, and you'll be fine. In fact, you'll be immune to catching any of the weightless viruses again. But if you are still floating by tomorrow morning, come back to see me, and we'll get you enrolled in some classes to help you deal with your new lifestyle."

"Anything I should do while I'm waiting to find out?" Jannette asked.

"Not really," Doctor Benson said. "Just relax. Probably best to stay home for the rest of the day, you know, just to avoid any accidents. As for urinating, many clients use the bathtub technique. They just fill their bathtub with water and get in the tub and urinate in the bath water. The urine gets diluted with the water and then bonds to the water molecules so that it doesn't float up out of the water."

"You mean I have to run a bath every time I pee?" Jannette asked.

"Well, most of my patients just keep their tub full, and add hot water if it gets too cold."

"You mean they get into a bathtub they've already peed in?!" Jannette asked incredulously.

"Actually Jannette, urine is sterile. It's not dirty," Dr. Benson replied.

"Oh, gross!" Jannette said.

"Well, in your case, maybe you should run a fresh tub each time. After all, it's probably only for today. My guess is that by tomorrow you'll be fine."

"I certainly hope so!" Jannette said.

She didn't have any more questions, so she thanked Dr. Benson and left his office.

When she got home, Jannette called her friend Amy and told her what had happened.

"Oh my God," Amy said. "That's horrible.... Wait...or is it a good thing?"

"I don't know," Jannette replied. "I was wondering that myself."

"There has to be some way to monetize this," Amy said.

"What do you mean?" Jannette asked.

"You know, monetize it—make money off it. That's the big thing today. You take something that you already have and you figure out how to sell it or sell advertising on it...you know, like people who make their car payments by putting ads on the car they're driving. Maybe you could figure out how to make millions off of being weightless."

"I hadn't thought about that," Jannette said.

They talked about other things for a while, but then Amy had to go. After they hung up, Jannette thought about Amy's suggestion. If she was going to be normal tomorrow, she would have to figure out something to do today to make money from being weightless. Maybe she could help open supermarkets by floating above them holding a big sign... or maybe she could get a job changing light bulbs at the top of those tall cell phone towers all over town...or maybe she could be a paparazzi and float over the houses of famous people and take pictures of them to sell...But every idea she thought of wouldn't work if she woke up with her normal weight tomorrow. Then she thought of the pee. Would the pee still be weightless tomorrow even if she wasn't? She wasn't sure. She hadn't asked her doctor that question. But if it did stay weightless, maybe she could make toys that float for children by filling very light plastic balls with her pee.

She wasn't sure if they would sell more than helium balloons, but she decided that she should save all her pee for the rest of the day. Besides, she might have a better idea tomorrow of how to monetize her pee.

So for the rest of the day, Jannette drank lots of water and tried to pee as often as she could. She got pretty good at aiming her pee and holding a ziplock bag low over the front of the toilet so that all the pee would flow directly up into the bag. By the time her bedtime rolled around, she had ten bags of pee floating above the floor in her bathroom. She swished them all into the closet and closed the door. She didn't want to accidentally step on them during the night. Then she went to bed. It was chilly that night, so she put an extra blanket on the bed.

That night, Jannette dreamed of all the different things she might make with weightless pee. Maybe she could make something artsy, like floating butterflies. She would have to figure out how to make a plastic bag in the shape of a butterfly and paint it pretty colors, and she would have to figure out how to get the pee into the butterfly bag and then seal it... maybe she would have to partner with some type of company that helped artsy inventors. Maybe she would have to talk with a lawyer about protecting her ideas.

Jannette woke up the next morning. She was all warm and snuggly under the covers. For a brief moment she forgot about how bizarre yesterday was, but then she remembered.

"I feel normal today," she thought. "I guess I just had the one-day virus."

She had to go to the bathroom. She threw off the covers and stepped out of bed, and floated up to the ceiling.

THE GOSPEL ACCORDING TO PHILIP

In 393 AD, at the Synod of Hippo, the Council of Bishops of the early Christian Church approved the first Christian Biblical Canon—the text that over the centuries became known as the Bible. The council decided which biblical stories were holy scripture and should be retained, and which should be removed. The following story by Philip the Apostle was removed from the New Testament by unanimous vote of the council.

And lo, as Jesus did descend from giving his sermon on Mount Eremos, a man dressed in the clothes of a beggar came unto Jesus and fell to his knees and did beseech Him, "Oh Lord Jesus, you are so great and powerful, and I am but a lowly poor outcast. Please, I beg you, have mercy upon me."

And Jesus smiled and placed his hand upon the poor man's shoulder, and said, "What is your name, my son?"

And the man looked about the multitude much afraid and whispered to Jesus, "My name is Chode."

And Jesus smiled again and asked, "What can I do for you, Chode?"

And Chode said, "Can you spare me two shekels, so that I may get to Jerusalem? I really need to get out of Galilee."

And Jesus said, "Why do you need to leave Galilee?"

"It's a long story, Lord. But if I stay here, I'm a dead man. I had this girlfriend, you see, and now she's in the family way."

And Jesus said, "If your woman is with child, you must do the right thing and marry her and support her, Chode."

And Chode replied, "Well, it's complicated, Lord. I would marry her, but I can't because I need her family's permission. She's only 15."

And Jesus removed his hand from Chode's shoulder and said, "And how old are you, Chode?"

And Chode replied, "I'm 38."

And Jesus said, "That's a pretty big age difference, Chode."

And Chode said, "Not my fault, Lord. She swore up and down she was 18."

And Jesus said, "Well Chode, you have sinned. You should go to her family and ask their forgiveness and ask permission to marry this child and provide for her."

And Chode replied, "I can't, Jesus. The family has vowed to kill me. That's why I need to get out of Galilee. I'm only two shekels short for a ride to Jerusalem."

And Jesus said, "Running away will not solve your problem, Chode. If the family will not allow you to marry the girl, you must give them a money offering and vow to pay them each month until their grandchild reaches the age of majority."

And Chode said, "Actually, Jesus, running away *will* solve my problem, because my problem is they want to kill me. And if I run away, I won't get killed. Besides, I have no money to give them."

And Jesus said, "Then you should get a job, Chode."

And Chode said, "I can't. I have a couple of convictions and you know how it is...no one wants to hire an ex-con."

And Jesus said, "What are your convictions for, Chode?"

And Chode said, "Oh, just minor stuff, Jesus. A couple of burglaries, an assault, several drunk-in-public misdemeanors. I'm a Samaritan, you see, and you know how it is with us Samaritans—we can't catch a break. Even the Jews hate us. Anyway, about those two shekels...If you could just see your way clear to loaning me two shekels, it would really save my life—and I mean that, literally. This girl's family is looking everywhere for me."

And Jesus said, "Well, Chode, you should go to the authorities and seek protection against this family if they are trying to harm you."

And Chode said, "I can't. I have this old warrant out of Nazareth and if I go to the authorities, they'll just arrest me. I just can't go back to prison, Lord."

And Jesus said, "It seems to me, Chode, that you have an excuse for everything. You can't catch a break because you are a Samaritan; you can't get a job because you have convictions; you got your girlfriend with child because she lied to you about her age; you can't marry her because you can't get her family's permission; you can't stay in Galilee because this family wants to kill you; you can't go to the authorities because you have an old warrant. Nothing is your fault. I hear a lot of excuses but no remorse."

And Chode said, "You're right, Lord. But I just don't want to die. I mean, it's a big family and they all really want to kill me. Do you know what it's like to have some group want to kill you? It's horrible. I just don't want to die."

And Jesus took pity on Chode, and said, "Look, Chode, I don't have any money, but you see that fellow standing over there with the brown cloak? That's Thomas, one of my disciples. He's always good for a couple of shekels. Go ask him."

And Chode said, "Thank you Jesus, thank you." And Chode stood up and went over to Thomas.

And the disciple James did approach Jesus and did say, "Oh Master, I could not but help but overhear that ...that man..."

"Yes," Jesus said, "he was an idiot. It is amazing, James, how some people just don't want to take responsibility for their lives. They walk around in a cloud, thinking that what they do and what happens to them are two totally separate things, but in reality they are two sides of the same shekel."

And James said, "That's good, Master. I shall have to add that to my journal. What a person does and what happens to them are two sides to the same shekel. Yes, I like that. You are truly wise, Master."

And Jesus said, "Thanks James, but we'd better get going. We've got a long way to go to get to Golgotha."

LOVE AND HIGGS BOSON

For some odd reason known only to the building's architects, the Fermilab's coffee shop was located underground, on the floor directly below the lab's neutron accelerator. The walls and ceiling of the coffee shop were not insulated enough to keep out the low hum of the nuclear generators that powered thousands of neutrons through a ninety-mile circular tunnel at speeds approaching the speed of light. Some of the newer scientists found the constant hum annoying, but the older scientists had long since gotten used to it and barely even noticed it.

Dr. Michael Zurich found Wilson Novi sitting in the coffee shop that Tuesday afternoon, sitting at his favorite table over in the corner, sitting alone, drinking decaffeinated coffee and staring into space. Dr. Zurich assumed that Dr. Novi was contemplating their current project, a complicated experiment involving splitting the same Higgs boson particle at different points in time as a way of testing whether Einstein's theory of the relative nature of time-gravity worked at the subatomic level. But in fact, Wilson Novi was thinking about his wife.

They had been married for five years. She was much younger than he, and he was suspicious that she was cheating on him. There wasn't anything he could put his finger on; no hard evidence. Jeannie wasn't treating him any differently…but he couldn't shake this nagging feeling that she was sharing her body with another man, letting someone else touch her naked flesh, squeeze her buttocks, kiss her breasts, finger her dark secrets, enter her and pound away inside her. The idea of another man's cock stretching out her wet vagina, squirting semen deep inside her—semen that would slowly drip out of her onto the towel that he imagined she had laid on top of their bed—infuriated Wilson. He imagined her taking a shower after her lover leaves, and then washing the towel she dries herself with and the towel from the bed, and then taking both towels from the dryer and folding them and placing them back on the linen shelf before he even got home in the evening. She was probably clever enough not to use any scented fabric softener in the dryer, so the towels wouldn't even smell freshly washed. She probably even placed them underneath all the other towels on the shelf. Last night, while Jeannie was in the kitchen making dinner, Wilson went to the linen closet and smelled all the towels, trying to detect a scent of fresh laundry soap, but they all just smelled like towels. He had no positive proof. He would just have to keep alert and observe, like any good scientist.

Wilson Novi was so deep in thought that he didn't even see Dr. Zurich walking up to his table.

"Ah, Dr. Novi," Michael Zurich said as he got to the table. "I am so sorry to disturb you, but Dr. Blair asked me to find you. He's made some new calculations that he shared with me this morning, and I have to say, they're very impressive. We ran some computer simulations, and his new formulas hold up even in the symmetric time simulation. He wants to alter our experiments with the Higgs boson particle so we can incorporate his new formulas into the model."

Wilson nodded without saying a word and stood up. Both men walked out of the coffee shop and back towards the lab without talking. Michael Zurich always found Dr. Novi's silent manner irritating. He respected someone who doesn't talk unless they have something important to say, but you'd think that after three years of working together that there would be some kind of chitchat, some kind of small talk. But Dr. Novi was the most taciturn, silent, passive man that Michael Zurich had ever met. No wonder Jeannie was bored to death in that marriage.

Michael Zurich was, of course, boning Jeannie on the side. His office had a private outside door, and about once a week he would slip away and drive over to Dr. Novi's house where Jeannie was waiting for him. God, what a magnificent body she had! She would lay down on that thick towel she placed over the bed, spread her legs and he would eat her out, sucking up those sweet juices that dribbled out of her vulva lips. Then he would mount her and thrust away, shooting hot sperm deep inside her. There was never much time for talk, because he had to get back to the lab, but it was an arrangement that worked out well for both of them. Dr. Zurich's own wife had long since stopped looking attractive to him, and Jeannie had come along just in the nick of time.

Carter Blair, the other PhD scientist in their lab, was also fucking Jeannie. Carter would sometimes cover for Michael when Michael was over at Jeannie's house, and Michael would sometimes make excuses for Carter's whereabouts when Carter was visiting Jeannie. Once, about a year ago, when Dr. Novi was out of town at a conference, Michael and Carter and Jeannie had a threesome. Michael was a little leery when Carter first brought the idea up, because Michael was afraid of any bisexual urges he might feel, but it turned out to be one of the hottest sex experiences he had ever had. It was rare for Dr. Novi to ever be away from the office, but he was awarded a coveted scientific award by the American Quantum Physics

Institute and had to travel to Chicago to receive it. Both Carter and Michael wanted to take advantage of Dr. Novi's absence to have extended sex time with Jeannie, but they couldn't agree on who should get the coveted time. Michael argued that he should get it because he was married and Carter was single, and thus Carter had more opportunity to find sex; but Carter argued that it was he who had nominated Dr. Novi for the award, for the specific purpose of getting him out of town, and thus he deserved the fruits of his efforts. They were at an impasse when Carter suggested, "Why don't we both go?"

"You mean like a morning-afternoon shift?" Michael asked.

"No, I mean at the same time," Carter explained.

"Uh, uh, I'm not gay," Michael sputtered.

"Neither am I," Carter retorted, "but we can still both do her, take turns, double penetration...come on, I'll ask her. I bet she'd love it."

And so she did. And so they all did. Michael Zurich never could understand what made that sex so hot. He wondered whether it was being able to feel Carter Blair's cock through Jeannie's vaginal wall when Carter was fucking her ass from behind while he was thrusting deep into her vagina, or whether it was the amazing sounds that Jeannie made when she orgasmed, not once but three times. Yes, that had been amazing sex. Unfortunately, Dr. Novi had not won any other awards since that time, so there had been no more threesomes.

Unbeknownst to Dr. Zurich, Carter Blair was also boning Charlene, Dr. Zurich's wife. Every Monday, both Dr. Novi and Dr. Zurich spent all day in the lab running their time symmetry experiments on the Higgs boson particles, so it was the perfect time for Dr. Blair to slip away and fuck Charlene. Charlene was not as animated as Jeannie, and she didn't like any ass play, but she was still a good fuck. Between Jeannie and Charlene, Carter was getting laid twice a week, and rarely had time or inclination to hit the bars looking for single ladies.

Dr. Blair had just printed out the computer projections of probable outcomes using his new calculations when Dr. Zurich and Dr. Novi walked into his office.

"Ah, you found him," Dr Blair said.

"Yes, in the coffee shop," responded Dr. Zurich.

"Excellent," Dr. Blair said, and then addressed Dr. Novi. "Something you said at our last staff meeting, doctor, about the instability of the particle wave measurements, got me thinking. What if it wasn't that the particle was unstable while shifting into a wave, but rather, that our method of measuring the shift was unstable? Let me show you."

Dr. Blair spread out his newly printed graphs on the small conference table in his office. As he spread the sheets of paper out, he was thinking about spreading Jeannie's legs apart, and adjusting them at just the right angle so that he could lower his head between her legs and lick those sweet pussy juices.

Dr. Novi watched Dr. Blair adjust each white sheet of paper carefully. It reminded him of the white towels, folded and stacked so carefully on the linen shelf...towels he knew were being used to protect the bedspread from evidence of Jeannie's cheating.

Dr. Zurich also gazed at the square sheets of paper on the table. They made him think of his mortgage payments. Seven more and the house would be paid off. Another reason not to divorce Charlene—he would have to give her half the house. As long as he could keep fucking Jeannie once a week, he could tolerate staying married to Charlene.

"In this first graph, we see the usual pattern we're accustomed to," Dr. Blair explained. "As soon as the Higgs boson shifts from a particle to a wave, the time symmetry measurement jumps on the graph, as if it were unstable. You see that spike at marker number four. But we know there is no loss of energy from the particle, so what is that spike actually evidence of?"

Dr. Novi wondered if he could mark the towels in a certain secret way, maybe place a tiny magic marker dot on the top towel in the morning right before he left for work. That way, if Jeannie washed the towel during the day and placed it at the bottom of the stack, he would be able to tell that night when he returned home. But even if the towel was moved, what would he do then? Maybe hire a private detective?

"The current Higgs boson theory is that there is one particle that shifts from matter to a wave, but I was wondering: what if there were two particles, and they were both shifting at the exact same moment in time?" Dr. Blair continued.

Or maybe, Dr. Novi thought, he could just take a drive home during the day, claim he had forgotten something, just walk in and see for himself what was going on.

"If the two particles were in opposite rotation, one existing as a wave and the other existing as a particle, each existing in different times at different locations, but being connected as if by a string...well, if they traded places, then their crossing paths, as it were, crossing paths at the same location and at the same moment in time...*that* could account for a spike in the time symmetry measurement, not because of a loss of energy, but because of the pressure of two events occurring at the same point in time where there was only sufficient time for one event. It happens so fast, because the wave is becoming a particle at exactly the same moment the particle is becoming a wave, but it's a sufficient disruption to register as if it were an energy increase, and thus we get this spike."

Dr. Zurich was trying to remember the last time he had actually had sex with Charlene. It would have been before he started seeing Jeannie, so that meant at least a year. Well, she didn't seem to mind. She never mentioned it. Women, Dr. Zurich thought, lose interest in sex at a certain age. Men don't. Lucky for him he had found Jeannie. But he wondered if he shouldn't try to fuck Charlene maybe once this year. No, he decided, let sleeping dogs lie.

"Now this second graph," Dr. Blair was saying, "is just a mathematical model, but it shows what the time symmetry differential would look like if you assumed there were two different particles, connected by string theory, but existing in two different times and two different locations. When they exchange places, you see how smooth the time symmetry differential is? There's no spike...because the formula has replaced the energy measurement with the time and location. I'm predicting that if we alter our particle accelerator experiments to assume two different Higgs boson particles existing in two different times but exchanging places on a regular basis, that the experiment outcomes would resemble this second graph."

Dr. Novi was still thinking about marking the towels with a tiny black dot, but his scientific brain was following Dr. Blair's explanation.

"Very interesting, Dr. Blair, very interesting," Dr. Novi said. "You're saying there could be two different particles each on different cycles but sharing the same point in time and space on a regular basis. Interesting."

Dr. Novi bent over the table to examine the graph more carefully. "Do you think that would be a stable relationship?" he asked.

"Yes, as long as the exchange happens in hypertime," Dr. Blair replied. "If the two particles were caught in the same location at the same time longer than that, there would be...there would be...well, that would be an anomaly...an impossibility...there would be an atomic explosion at the sub-atomic level...but that has never happened."

"Not that we know of," Dr. Novi replied. "Maybe it happens all the time, tiny sub-atomic explosions...destroying sub-atomic worlds...well, I'm just musing. What are these other charts?"

"Well, Dr. Novi," Dr. Blair said, "I got to wondering what would the measurements look like if they're were not just two particles, but three or four, all exchanging places at the same time on a different schedule, and the computer generated these graphs, but I haven't finished those calculations.

"Ah, I see," Dr. Novi said. "But I take it you want to modify the particle experiments to incorporate the calculations underlying this second chart?"

"Yes, sir," Dr. Blair said, "that was my hope."

"I think we can accommodate that. Why don't you write up a proposal and let's review it at the next staff meeting."

"Thank you, sir," Dr. Blair said.

Dr. Novi picked up the second chart and studied it. "Yes, very interesting. Two particles in different locations but sharing the same point in time at an identical location on some type of schedule...interesting...almost like two lovers sharing the same woman...hmm. Good work, Dr. Blair."

And with that, Dr. Novi shuffled out of the room, still holding the second page in his hand and looking at it. After the door closed, Dr. Zurich turned to Dr. Blair and asked, "Do you think he knows?"

"No way," Dr. Blair replied. "He's lost in his own world."

At that exact moment in time, Jeannie was slipping into bed with Tom, her next door neighbor. Whenever Tom's wife was out of town at a book convention, Tom would drop by for a quickie.

THE PROBLEM WITH
THE LACK OF PAY PHONES

There used to be pay phones on every corner...you know, back before everyone carried a cell phone in their pocket. You could always find a pay phone, drop a dime in, and make a call...yeah a dime, that's all it cost, a lousy dime.

I remember I used to go to the pay phones all the time and call up God. My aunt gave me his number, just before she passed away. I kept it on a piece of paper in my wallet. She told me it was a special number that went directly to God.

So whenever I had a question, I would just call him up, and ask him my question. He always answered on the second ring. Never the first ring. Always the second ring. I would call up and say things like, "There's this girl in my class that I really like, but I'm scared to talk with her", and he would give me real good advice, like "Just ask her to help you with one math problem from class," or something like that. It's funny—his advice was always practical, never spiritual or any of that shit. I mean, he never told me to pray or nothin'.

He would just give me a practical suggestion.

I remember one time, when my parents were getting divorced, and they asked me who I wanted to live with, and I didn't know, because I loved them both...but they kept pressuring me to choose, and told me that I had to tell the judge when we went to court. So the night before court, I snuck out of the house and found a pay phone and called God, and he was so smart. He told me to look the judge straight in the eye and tell him I loved both my parents so much and I wanted to live with both of them, and then to cry as loud as I could. And you know what? It worked. The judge took my parents into some back room, and when they came out, they said they weren't going to get divorced that day after all. So we all went back home. And they never did get divorced. I think God somehow helped them figure out how to put up with each other.

I wish there were more pay phones. You can't call God on a cell phone, you know. It has to be a pay phone. Sometimes, when I run across some old pay phone, like in the back of a gas station or somewhere, I put some coins in and call up God, just for old times' sake, and tell him I'm doing okay. He likes to hear that, you know...he likes to hear that people are doing okay, that his advice was good. I bet it gets lonely up there, what with there not being so many pay phones and all. I bet he gets a lot fewer calls these days.

HOW TOBY LEARNED TO KEEP HIS MOUTH SHUT

It wasn't a particularly sunny day. There was a thin layer of clouds that diffused the sunlight enough to call it a cloudy day. But it was still bright enough that Toby needed sunglasses. Tacoma was like that: always overcast but with a lot of glare. It was annoying. Plus, Toby was hungry. He walked along the sidewalk looking for a place to eat that wasn't too crowded. He wasn't picky about the food, but he didn't want to wait to get a table.

He headed toward the Subs and Suds Café on Fourth Avenue. That was always a good place to get a sandwich and a beer, and it was rarely crowded. He wove his way through the people on the sidewalk, irritated at how the slowest walkers always hogged the middle of the sidewalk instead of plodding along on one side or the other. He thought that sidewalks ought to be marked with slow and fast lanes the same way as streets were. An older couple was just ahead of him. He veered left to pass them. As he did, he walked close by a fat, disheveled woman sitting on the window ledge of a closed art store.

"Do you have an extra dollar?" she asked him as he walked by.

"Sorry," he said and kept moving. He had seen this woman many times over the years. She was one of the many homeless who hung around Fourth Avenue, panhandling, hassling tourists and residents, always asking for a dollar. Her face was round and red with rosacea. More likely from alcohol, Toby thought. Like so many other vagrants, she lived on the street—sleeping in alleys, parks—God knows where. Her clothes were filthy. Toby didn't want to walk too close to her because he didn't want to get a sniff of how she must smell. But he needed to pass that old couple, so he picked up his pace. There was a man in a hooded sweatshirt, standing in the doorway of the art store next to her.

"Come on man, give my woman a dollar," the man suddenly said.

Toby kept moving, past both of them, saying nothing, not looking at either one. God, he hated panhandlers. Why doesn't the city pass a "no soliciting" ordinance like so many other cities? It was ridiculous.

He kept walking, weaving through the crowd. The sun peeked out and then went back behind the clouds. He crossed the street and kept moving. On the next block he got to Subs and Suds. He looked in the window—lots of open tables. Good, he thought, and stepped inside.

Familiar restaurant sounds and smells enveloped him. He quickly took a seat at a small booth against the wall. He looked at the menu for a bit, but he already knew what he wanted. Toby was the kind of guy who, once he found something that he liked at a restaurant, he would always order the same meal on every subsequent visit. And at the Subs and Suds, Toby always ordered the Tombstone Sandwich on sourdough bread. It was his favorite: roast beef, turkey, bacon, tomato, and avocado, with jalapeño sauce. He looked around—where was the waitress? The place wasn't that busy—he should at least have water by now. A young Latino was clearing a nearby table. Toby waved at him. The lad put his tray down and came over to Toby.

"Yes sir?" he asked.

"Could I get a Tombstone Sandwich on sourdough?" Toby said.

"I'll get your waitress," the busboy said and turned away.

"Could I at least get some water?" Toby asked as the lad walked off without responding.

Jesus, Toby thought to himself—it's not that complicated of an order. A simple Tombstone Sandwich.

He watched the busboy talk to a waitress who then came over to Toby's table.

"Ready to order?" the waitress asked.

"Yes," said Toby, feeling irritated. "I'd like a Tombstone Sandwich on sourdough.

"Chips or fries?" the waitress asked cheerfully.

"Uh...chips I guess," Toby said.

"And to drink?"

"Just water," Toby said, looking away.

"It comes with a soda," the waitress said, still being cheerful.

"Yeah, okay. Fine, I'll have a diet coke."

The waitress left to put the order in. Toby guessed she was being extra cheerful just to irritate him. Jesus, he just wanted to eat! He should have had more for breakfast than just that banana.

The waitress returned with a large cup and put it on Toby's table. He looked at it. It was empty.

"What's this?" he asked the waitress.

"We got a new soda machine," she replied, still in that cheerful voice. She pointed to a soda machine on the table in the corner. "Help yourself." And she walked away.

Good God almighty, Toby thought. I just wanted a glass of water! He pulled himself out of the tiny booth and walked over to the soda machine. He filled his cup with diet coke, then saw the ice dispenser. When he pressed the lever, the ice fell into his cup with such force that it splashed coke all over his hands.

Goddamnit, he thought. He shook the coke off his hand, refilled his cup, looked around for a napkin dispenser but saw none. He walked back to his table, but there was no napkin dispenser there either. He walked up to the counter. One young man was preparing sandwiches while another was working the grill.

"Can I have some napkins, please?" Toby asked.

The young man pointed to a napkin dispenser on the counter. Toby scowled and pulled a thick wad of paper napkins out and wiped his hands.

There's just no customer service anywhere, he thought to himself, and walked back to his table. Even at the neighborhood sandwich shop, there's no concept of good customer service. How do they expect to earn repeat business? Back in his day, a waitress would bring you water and napkins the second you sat down. And they were friendly, not fake cheerful. And if you had to ask a busboy for something, the manager himself would come over and make sure you were being taken care of. Those days are gone, Toby thought. He dried his hands, wadded the napkins up and placed them on the table. He looked around. No wonder there were always open tables at this joint. Probably because no one ever comes back.

He sighed and thought about other things for a while. His back hurt. These small booths never have enough padding, he thought. He took a sip of his diet coke. It was flat.

Just then the waitress brought a plastic tray over to him with his sandwich and a bag of potato chips. It looked good, but the bread seemed too white.

"Is this sourdough?" he asked her.

"No, we're out of sourdough. Sorry," she said and walked away.

That's it, he thought to himself—I'm not coming back here.

He took a bite of the sandwich. Even with white bread, it was still good...mostly because he was so hungry.

While he ate, he thought about his day. It wasn't a particularly memorable day. He had had a hard time getting out of bed, and he ended up having to rush to make it to work on time. That was why he only had time to grab a banana as he left his apartment. But time had seemed to slow down at work that morning. It had been an annoying morning at work. But as he munched on his sandwich and thought about it, he couldn't remember why it had been annoying. In fact, he couldn't remember much about his morning...only that he hated his job.

As he finished the last bite of his sandwich, some fat guy with food stains on his shirt came up to his table. His name tag indicated he was some kind of manager.

"How was everything, sir?" the man asked.

Toby wiped his mouth and then said, "Well, I would have liked the sandwich on sourdough bread the way I ordered it. And I don't like your new self-service coke machine—it spilled coke all over me.... And I had to ask the busboy to find a waitress so I could order lunch." Toby smiled a slightly malevolent smile, and then added, "But other than that, it was okay."

The fat manager seemed taken aback by Toby's directness. He frowned and walked away and talked with the waitress, and then with the cook before returning to Toby's table.

"I'm very sorry sir. Apparently we ran out of sourdough bread, and the fountain drink machine is new. I've taken care of your check. Your meal is on the house. We hope you come back."

Toby was surprised, but pleased to get a free meal. "Yes, well thank you...yes I will," Toby said.

The manager walked away. Toby saw the waitress was

glaring at him from across the room. He thought to himself that if he ever did come back here, she would probably spit in his food. No, he decided, he would not come back here.

As he walked out the front door, he thought again how lucky he was that he got to eat lunch for free. He was proud of himself for speaking up.

He started to walk back towards his office.

"Do you have an extra dollar?"

He looked over to his right. It was that same red-faced homeless woman. She must have lugged herself up the street to find a better corner to panhandle on. Her sweatshirt-wearing boyfriend was a few feet away, sitting on the curb next to her with the hood still over his head.

"No, I don't," he said.

"Maybe some extra change so I can get something to eat?" she asked, and stepped towards him.

"No, sorry," Toby said, and moved to step around her.

But she stepped in front of him and said, "I saw you eating in there. I'm hungry. Can't you spare a dollar?"

Toby was offended that she was blocking his way and being so aggressive. He glared at her and said, "I said no! Look, I see you on this street all the time, always begging for money. I don't have any money to give you!"

"I just need a dollar or two so I can get something to eat," the woman said. "Can't you help me out?"

"No!" Toby screamed. "I didn't put you in this situation! It's not my job to get you out of your mess! Go get a job, or get on unemployment, or do whatever you people do, but stop bothering me. I don't have any money for you! Just leave me alone!" And he stepped around her and continued up the street. His face was flushed with anger. He couldn't believe the streets were so bad that he had to yell at panhandlers to leave him alone.

Toby never saw who picked up the rock and threw it

at him. As he later told the policeman while the ambulance attendants were dressing his wound, the woman accosted him and he had simply told her to stop and had walked away; and the next thing he knew, about half a block away, he was lying on the sidewalk with the worst pain in his head that he had ever felt in his life, and blood running down the side of his face. His back was to the woman and her boyfriend when the rock was thrown, so he couldn't be sure who threw it. Besides, he never got a good look at the man in the hooded sweatshirt.

The policeman carefully wrote down what Toby said. Then he closed his notebook and told Toby that they would investigate the case and try to find any eyewitnesses.

As the two ambulance attendants helped Toby into the ambulance, one of them mentioned to the other that he had noticed there were a lot more mentally ill homeless on the street these days. The other attendant nodded his head in agreement and added that you could never tell what might set them off.

FEELING SPECIAL?

It was Gabriel who told the other angels, "Look, we have got to talk to God about this." The other angels were afraid of God (you know how He can be), but they all agreed, provided that Gabriel would be their spokesman.

So Gabriel made an appointment, and a week later he was ushered into God's conference room.

God was seated, as usual, in a beautiful throne behind a huge mahogany table. The grain in the wood gleamed and caught Gabriel's eye.

"Nice table, God," Gabriel said.

"Thanks," God said.

"What is it?"

"It's mahogany," God said. "From trees. I just created it... wonderful wood, very pretty, very suitable for furniture. I'm going to plant it around that equator thing on Earth."

"Nice," Gabriel said.

"Well, you didn't come here to talk about furniture," God said. "What can I do for you today, Gabriel?"

"Speaking of Earth, God," Gabriel started, "it's about

those human beings you created in your image, you know, Adam and Eve and all the rest..."

"Yes, aren't they wonderful?" God said.

"Yes, well, about them...we...I mean, me and the other angels, we're concerned that they are a bit too much in your own image."

"What do you mean?" God asked.

"Well, it's about this consciousness thing. You gave them a lot of that, you know. They're like, well, they're like aware of *everything*."

"Yes..." God said, "and what's the problem with that?"

"Well, to be perfectly frank, God, they're a bit too much like little gods. They have divine consciousness and see how they're totally connected to all living things...and they understand karma and see how their actions affect all other creatures. The other angels are kind of worried they're going to...well, that they're going to replace us angels."

"Well, Gabriel," God interrupted. "I gave them death! After you all complained the last time, I created death so they wouldn't take over the heavens. In fact, at the rate they're going, they can't reproduce enough to even populate the earth. What more do you want?"

"Yes, well, about that, God...one of the angels, Satan, has developed a lobe that we would like you put in these humans."

"Satan, huh?" said God, rubbing his chin. "What's he up to this time?"

"Well, actually, God, the other angels and I think this idea makes some sense. All it is, is a small prefrontal lobe that could be put in the humans' brains—it wouldn't take up hardly any room, and it wouldn't alter their physiology. Satan calls it an NTBS lobe."

"Yeah?" said God, "and what does that stand for?"

"Need To Be Special," answered Gabriel. "This NTBS lobe doesn't change anything about their consciousness, but it does make them think about themselves first. It's a subtle shift. Whenever they perceive something, they'll still be able to think about how it affects everyone else, but the first thought they'll have will be how it affects themselves."

"Uh huh," said God. "That doesn't seem so special. What else does it do?"

"Well, it makes them yearn," Gabriel admitted.

"Yearn?" asked God, "What is that?"

"It's like a low-grade desire," Gabriel explained. "They will always yearn to be special."

"I don't follow," said God. "Give me some examples."

"Well, for example, Eve might look at her reflection and think she needs a new hat, to stand out as different—as special—from the other women."

"What's a hat?" God asked.

"It's a pretty thing you put on your head. Michael is working on a whole concept called clothes, which are pretty things humans can put on their bodies."

"Oh, ok," said God, "So give me more examples of what this NTBS lobe does."

"It's very simple, really. It just always makes them want to be special, to stand out as different from the others..."

"Does it make them want to be better humans?" God interrupted.

"Well, kind of...it makes them want to appear as more important, as more valued."

God stroked his beard. "Interesting," he said. "It might play into this idea I've been having lately about sin and free will...interesting. You say this was Satan's idea?"

"Yes, he came up with it."

"You know, Gabriel," God said, "just between you and me, I don't always trust that Satan angel, but I must admit he comes up with some interesting ideas. The whole concept of evil was his idea, you know. I'm still not sold on that one, but I kind of like this one....Still, I want you to keep your eye on him. I don't need any upstarts in the angel choir, you know."

"Yes sir," Gabriel said.

"So what is the cost factor involved installing this NTBS lobe in the humans' brains?" God asked.

Gabriel pulled out some charts. "It's a net-zero cost, God. If we pull the energy from their metabolism, and offset that by increasing their sleep pattern by an additional four hours, we can install the NTBS lobes for no additional cost."

"How long will they need to sleep then, in total, to replenish their energy?" God asked.

"At least eight hours a day," Gabriel answered, looking at the chart, "nine preferably."

"I'd have to increase the day to 24 hours," God added, raising one eyebrow.

"Yes, we know," Gabriel said.

"You realize what that does?" God asked.

"Yes, we calculated that equation," Gabriel said. "It shortens the length of the entire universe to 13.82 billion years."

"Uh huh," God said. He sat back in this throne and thought about it for a bit, then asked, "So when would the universe end? I mean, when would it end in earth time?"

Gabriel looked at his charts. "In earth time?...Well, we calculate that increasing a day to twenty four hours would cause the universe to implode in what the humans will end up calling year 2025."

God stroked his beard and stared at the clouds by his feet. "Well, that's a pretty good run for this universe, don't you think, Gabriel? I mean 13.82 billion years. Just a blink of an eye, really. Maybe it'll generate some good data for the next universe. Yeah, I like the concept....Ok, let's do it. Start putting this NTBS lobe in the humans' brains. Keep me posted on how that proceeds."

"Thank you, God," Gabriel said, preparing to leave. "We'll get on it right away. I think it's a good plan. Thank you."

TRIGGERS

As soon as he sat down in Dr. Wilson's office, Lyle started talking.

"I had a close call the other day, Doc," he said. "It kinda scared me."

"What happened?" Dr. Wilson asked, opening his notepad.

"Well, I needed to go downtown, to do some shopping, and I had left my apartment and started walking, when it began to rain. But then a 159 bus came by—you know, the free ones that run downtown—so I hopped on it, so I wouldn't get wet...."

"What day was this?" Dr. Wilson asked, interrupting Lyle.

"Um, Tuesday...the day before yesterday."

Dr. Wilson frowned. "I don't recall it raining Tuesday, Lyle," he said.

"Well, these black clouds were rolling in, and it looked like rain, and I didn't want to get wet, so I..."

"Lyle, I remember Tuesday very well. It was a little cloudy, but no more than usual. There were no black clouds," Dr. Wilson said.

"Well, Doc, I was thinking it was going to rain...I mean, it looked liked rain to me..."

"So you hopped on a bus?" Dr. Wilson asked, frowning.

"Uh huh, yeah, yeah I did, 'cause I figured it was only for eight or nine blocks, I figured I could handle it," Lyle said.

"Well, Lyle, we've talked about this before. Riding on buses is a no-no. There are too many triggers for you."

"Yeah, I know," Lyle said. "But anyway, I was on the bus, and I didn't think it was going to be crowded, but it was..."

Dr. Wilson interrupted Lyle again. "I think I know where this is going, Lyle. So let's talk about it for a minute. As I recall, you live on Oak Street, just on the edge of downtown, right?"

Lyle nodded his head.

"So what alternatives would you have had to getting on the bus?" Dr. Wilson asked.

Lyle thought for a minute. "Well, I could have caught a cab, but I didn't have any money," he said.

"A cab? To ride eight or nine blocks?"

"Well, I didn't want to get wet."

"It didn't rain Tuesday, Lyle," Dr. Wilson said firmly.

"I guess I could have walked," Lyle said, his voice trailing off.

"What else?" Dr. Wilson asked.

Lyle frowned, then his eyes lit up. "I could have gone back to get an umbrella?"

"Right," said Dr. Wilson. "By the way, why were you going downtown?"

"To do some shopping," Lyle answered.

"For...?"

"Just window shopping," Lyle said. "I just wanted to get out of the apartment."

"Why did you want to get out of the apartment?" Dr. Wilson asked.

"Well, you know, I get feeling cooped up there," Lyle said.

"I see," said Dr. Wilson. "So, you started feeling cooped

up in your apartment—feeling anxious, right? So that's a trigger...What were you doing in your apartment that led to you feeling cooped up?"

Lyle lowered his head. "Well, I was watching some videos..."

"You were watching porn again, right?" Dr. Wilson asked.

Lyle just nodded his head yes.

"Ok, well, we have several triggers here, Lyle. You were watching porn on your computer...we've talked about that before. So you know that's always a trigger...and so you got sexually aroused...and then you started feeling anxious...another trigger...so you went for a walk on some excuse to do some window shopping, but you got on a bus right away, on the excuse that it might rain...am I getting all this right, Lyle?"

Lyle pursed his lips and nodded yes.

"And let me guess..." Dr. Wilson continued. "The bus was crowded and there were some women on the bus, right?"

Again, Lyle nodded his head.

"So what happened?"

"Well, there was this woman there on the bus. It was crowded so she was standing, you know, holding onto one of those bars, and her arm was up, and I could see she didn't shave her armpits, 'cause her blouse had no sleeves, and that got me excited, and I could see her bra and where her skin went under her bra..."

"And you spotted this woman right away?" Dr. Wilson asked.

"Oh yeah, as soon as I got on the bus. And I tried to look away, but I couldn't, and I kinda made my way closer, and, you know, and I didn't want to, but I got real close, and I could smell her, and I wanted to get closer, but then this guy—I think it may have been her boyfriend—he gave me a mean look and he stepped between me and her...and by then I was downtown, and he kept staring at me, so I got off the bus..."

"Hmmm, well, he did you a big favor, Lyle," Dr. Wilson said.

Lyle just nodded.

"What would you have done if he hadn't been there, Lyle?" Dr. Wilson asked.

"Nothing, nothing, I swear, Doc. I just wanted to get closer to her."

"Uh huh...well, I think you would have tried to rub against her, wouldn't you have?"

Lyle looked like he was about to cry. "When I got off the bus, Doc, I was shaking. I felt ashamed again."

"Look, Lyle. If you put yourself in those situations, you're going to re-offend. We've talked about this. Once you get that far in the sequence, you don't have enough willpower to stop. The only way you can get control of this addiction is not to put yourself in that situation. You cannot ride on buses. And you shouldn't watch pornography, but if you're going to watch porn, you've got to masturbate right away, to relieve the tension—you can't just watch pornography and then go get on a bus."

Lyle opened his mouth as if he was going to say something, but then closed his mouth and nodded.

Dr. Wilson continued, "This sequence always follows the same pattern: You're alone; you're bored; you watch porn; you get excited; you go out and get on a bus; you see someone and you get aroused; you try to rub against them; and then you get ashamed...." Dr. Wilson paused. "You don't want to go back to prison, do you?"

Tears started to roll down Lyle's cheeks. He shook his head no.

"Ok, I don't want you to either, Lyle...How's the journal writing coming along?"

"Pretty good, I guess," Lyle said.

"When you were home in your apartment, before you started watching pornography, did you write in your journal?"

Lyle shook his head no.

"Well, you see, Lyle, that's exactly the time that you need to start writing in your journal. One of the main benefits of keeping a journal is that it breaks the sequence. It engages your good brain, so you can see what the pattern is. You were home alone, and you were feeling bored, so you got online and watched some porn, right? But if you had opened your journal instead and started writing, you could have broken that sequential thinking...because when you get bored, that's the danger time—that's when you start watching porn. So that's when you need to start writing in your journal instead."

Lyle nodded his head in agreement.

"Did you bring your journal with you today?"

Lyle shook his head no.

"I want you to bring it every session, Lyle. Are you still going to the SAA groups?" Dr. Wilson asked.

"Yes, I have group tonight," Lyle said.

"How many times a week do you go?" Dr. Wilson asked.

"Twice."

Dr. Wilson nodded and thought for a minute. "I think you need to up it to three times a week. Can you do that?"

Lyle nodded yes.

"Okay, good," Dr. Wilson said. "And the next time you come in to see me, I want you to bring your journal, okay?"

Lyle nodded.

"Alright, that's all we have time for today, Lyle."

Lyle stood up to leave. Dr. Wilson added, "No more buses between now and when you come back to see me, understand?"

"Yes," Lyle said, "I understand. Thanks, Doc."

And he left.

Dr. Wilson made a few more notes in his notebook. He put his pen down and shook his head. He didn't have much hope for Lyle. His impulse control was so low. Dr. Wilson thought that it would just be a matter of time before Lyle re-offended and got arrested on a probation violation and sent back to prison. It was sad. Many of Dr. Wilson's patients were court-ordered to see him, and many of them just couldn't learn to identify what triggered their compulsions. If they could just learn to identify the triggers, Dr. Wilson thought, he could help them expand their range of behavioral alternatives...to make better choices...but so many of his patients were like Lyle—they just didn't seem to have the insight to get to that first step of seeing what triggered their compulsion.

Dr. Wilson looked at his watch. He had thirty minutes before his next patient. He put down his notebook, stood up, and went to the small bathroom on the side of his office and washed his hands. Then he closed and locked the door, unzipped his pants, pulled out his cock, and began to masturbate into the sink.

DUCK DUCK DRAKE

Drake Duck limped into the bar and ordered a beer.

"That'll be three dollars," said the bartender, placing a frothy glass of beer in front of Drake.

"Just put it on my bill," said Drake.

"What?" the bartender said.

"Sorry," said Drake. "Private joke." He pulled out his wallet and handed the bartender a five dollar bill.

Drake took a sip of his beer. It was good and cold. The bartender came back and placed Drake's two dollars of change on the bar. Drake picked up one bill, and gestured that the bartender could have the other.

"Thanks," said the bartender. Then the bartender looked at Drake's shirt and asked, "What's with the feathers?"

"It's my girlfriend's idea," Drake said. "Kinda like a down jacket without the jacket. She sews the calamus of each feather onto a cloth, like a cape, that snaps over a shirt..."

"The what of each feather?" the bartender asked.

"The calamus—that's the hollow shaft of a feather, like a quill," Drake said.

"Oh," the bartender said, then added, "What's a quill?"

"Look here," Drake said, pointing to his arm. "This part is the calamus—it's a hollow tube that gives the feather structure, but it's also flexible. This whole part is called the vane; this part where the calamus gets smaller is called the rachis."

"Uh huh, well, you know a lot about feathers," the bartender said.

"Well...I'm a duck," Drake said.

"What?" the bartender asked.

"Sorry. Another private joke," Drake said.

"So anyway," the bartender continued. "What's the deal, though? I mean, why feathers?"

"Well, like I said, it's my girlfriend's project," Drake explained. "She designs clothes. She had the idea for a lightweight down jacket that was more stylish than those typical puffy jackets that make you look like the Michelin Man. Those jackets, you know, are basically just tubes. They fill the tubes with loose feathers and sew the tubes together to form a jacket. That's why they're so bulky—you're basically wearing a balloon of tubes. So she started looking at how birds actually wear feathers. They're not loose, obviously—they overlap in patterns. They still trap air, so they're warm. But they're not bulky. Most birds actually have three or four layers of feathers, but each layer is less than a millimeter thick. So anyway, she finished this jacket this morning and asked me to wear it around today to see how it worked."

"And?" the bartender asked.

"Well, I have to admit, it keeps me warm, and it's lightweight—perfect for this cold weather we've been having lately."

"Huh...so you like it?" the bartender asked.

"I like how it works, but I hate the design."

"You hate it?" the bartender asked.

"I hate the design. I mean, it's got feathers. It's the first thing you asked about when I sat down, right? It's a coat of feathers. Who wants to wear feathers?"

"A duck?" the bartender suggested.

"Exactly," Drake sighed and shook his head.

"What do you mean?" the bartender asked.

"It's my last name...Duck. All my life I've been teased for it. So the last thing I want to do is wear something that reminds me of my name."

"Your last name is Duck?" the bartender asked.

"Yeah."

"What's your first name?"

"Drake."

"Drake? Isn't that a type of duck?" the bartender asked.

"Yup," Drake said. "It's a male duck. My parents thought it was cute. My older brother had it worse. They named him Donald. He finally committed suicide. I have a younger brother who was originally named Mallard, but he went to court and had it changed to George."

"Wow," said the bartender.

"Yeah," said Drake, "parents can be idiots and do shit that really fucks up their kids."

"Tell me about it," the bartender said. "My parents named me Harry."

"What's wrong with that?" Drake asked.

"My last name is Peters."

"Harry Pet...oh I see," said Drake.

"Yeah."

"Well Harry, glad to meet you," Drake said extending his hand.

The bartender shook Drake's hand and said, "Glad to meet you, Drake. Are you from around here?"

"No," Drake said. "My girlfriend and I are from Canada. We're just passing through...staying with some friends for a few days before we fly out tomorrow."

"Where you heading?"

"We go south each winter," Drake said. "We rent a condo in Baja, California, and stay until spring."

"Nice," the bartender said. "You speak Spanish?"

"Naaa, don't need to. Everyone there is from Canada or the U.S."

"Snowbirds, huh?...oh, sorry," the bartender said.

"It's okay," Drake said. "I'm used to it."

"Want another beer?"

"Yeah, sure," Drake said. "You got a bathroom here?"

"Yeah, it's in the back," the bartender said, taking Drake's glass. "They're doing some construction back there, so just watch your head stepping through the door."

"Thanks," Drake said, and got up from the barstool where he had been sitting and slowly limped across the floor. The bartender gave him a concerned look.

"Twisted my ankle this morning," Drake explained.

The bartender nodded and turned his attention to refilling Drake's glass. When the glass was full, he knocked the extra form off with a wooden foam scraper and placed the beer on the bar in front of where Drake had been sitting.

Drake limped back to his chair a few minutes later.

"Would you be more comfortable in one of the booths?" the bartender asked

"Naaa, I'm fine here," Drake said, reaching for his wallet.

"That's all right," the bartender said, waving his hand. "On the house."

"Hey, thanks, 'preciate that."

"You know, the regulars in this bar are kinda superstitious," the bartender said. "They won't sit in that seat."

"Why not?"

"Back in 1973, a fellow got shot from behind while sitting there. That seat puts your back to the front door—makes you an easy target."

Drake turned around, looked at the front door and said, "Yeah," he said. "I can see that. You get many shootings here?"

"No, just that one. But like I say, people here are superstitious."

"You know, Harry," Drake said. "I think I will move over to a booth. I might be more comfortable."

As Drake was standing up to move, one of the bar's regulars, Tony Palomino, came in and took a seat at the other end of the bar.

"Why the long face, Tony?" the bartender asked.

"Oh, don't start," Tony said with a scowl.

RIMM'S CREMATORIUM

Phil Rimm was on the phone with Mrs. Phelps.

"Yes, Mrs. Phelps, this Saturday? Ah, yes, I understand... With such short notice, Mrs. Phelps, I'm worried that if we mail the urn to you, it might not arrive in time. If you like, we could deliver it to you this afternoon—there's only a slight extra charge for that...Yes, alright, we'll do that then, say about three o'clock?...Yes, we have your address...Yes, well, I am so glad you found a captain who can sail to Mr. Phelps' favorite fishing spot. I think he would have been pleased. Plus, you'll have good weather for the service...Yes, yes, well, you're very welcome. We'll see you at three...Yes, goodbye."

Phil hung up the phone, and thought to himself: "What an annoying bitch."

He looked at his computer screen and opened the "client" folder and scrolled down to "Phelps" to find what urn model she had paid for. Then, he picked up the phone and called Jacob's extension.

"Hey Jacob, it's Phil. Can you do an urn delivery at three this afternoon?... Good. It's urn model 315—you know, the blue one with the gold trim? It's that Phelps woman. She's finally going to spread her husband's ashes at sea...well, not exactly at sea, but over at Swindle Lake at her husband's favorite fishing spot...Ha! Yeah, I know. It's ironic to think that the fish will be eating the remains of the man who once ate them. Yeah, well, that probably hasn't occurred to her... No, I'm not sorry to lose that account—she was such a nag. I swear, she has called me at least once a week since her husband died and that's been—what?—two years ago. She wasn't worth the monthly fee she paid. What a whiny bitch. No wonder her husband died... Anyway, take the small black sedan—it's in the garage. And wear the dark blue uniform. And don't forget to look somber... Ha! Yeah I know."

Jacob hung up the phone, closed out of the online poker game he had been playing, and got up from his desk and walked down the hallway to the urn room. It took him a minute to find the #315 shelf. They were only a few boxes left of that model. He made a mental note to order more. Then he took the empty urn down to the basement to the room marked "Authorized Personnel Only." He and Phil had the only keys. That's where they kept the large metal ash bin. He unlocked the door and went over to the ash bin, carefully lifted the cover to avoid creating air movement, and gently scooped up ashes with the blue urn. As soon as the urn was three-fourths full, Jacob lowered the cover on the ash bin, and screwed the lid of the urn on tight. Then he carefully wiped the outside of the urn clean of any loose ash, and took the urn back to his office.

It had been Phil's idea originally to mix all the cremated ashes into one large metal bin. When Phil's dad was alive, that would have never been permitted. But, like Phil always said, his dad had no business sense. After his dad died, Phil totally redesigned the company, and took it from a barely surviving family crematorium to a thriving business. It was like resurrecting a corpse, Phil always said. The business leaders in town credited Phil's hard work and tasteful advertising, but Jacob understood that it was a combination of the kickbacks Phil paid to the local mortuaries and his ability to cut costs. The biggest costs in the cremation business were in the individual cremations. The huge cremation furnace had to be heated to 1800 degrees—all for one body. Not only did it take almost three hours to cremate a body, but it took several hours for the furnace to cool down enough to open it and retrieve the ashes. Back in Phil's dad's day, the crematorium couldn't handle more than one cremation a day. That meant that Phil's dad lost a lot of business. If a family wanted a body cremated but didn't want to pay for embalming, state law required that the deceased had to be cremated within forty-eight hours of death. If the furnace wasn't available, Phil's dad would lose that business to some other crematorium in the county. That used to irk the shit out of Phil, especially because the family business was near a treacherously curvy state highway where there were a lot of accidents, sometimes with multiple fatalities. But when that happened, Rimm's could only get one of the bodies for cremation. The rest went to competitors. Back in the day, the most Phil could do to increase business was to go out on Saturday nights and shoot out the lights over the highway. But after Phil's dad died, Phil really streamlined the business. Instead of individual cremations, Phil and Jacob would just keep the bodies on ice until there were enough bodies to fill the furnace completely. All the ashes were dumped into the large metal ashbin in the basement. Phil would "schedule" a cremation whenever the bereaved family wanted it done, and deliver a full urn of ashes on time as promised. But the actual deceased might not get cremated until days or weeks later, depending on business. And the ashes that were given to the family were a mixture of whomever had been cremated recently. The cost savings was enormous, and Phil put those profits into conservative but prominent advertising, which just created more business.

Jacob took the urn back to his office, placed it on his desk and went to the closet to find one of the crematorium's standard dark blue uniforms.

*   *   *

It was the following week, on a Friday morning, when Darlene Bodine's body arrived. It's not that no one could have predicted that—Darlene probably consumed more drugs during her short twenty-six year-old life than most hardcore junkies twice her age. She was the town's crazy druggie party girl—at the bars, at the raves, in countless backseats of cars or motel rooms. "I'll blow any bloke for a line of coke" was her war cry. And the blokes all poured those lines out for her—because she was pretty and she had those full bouncy breasts that she loved to jiggle in front of men. So the fact that her last overdose did her in came as no surprise to anyone in town—although most expected her to last a few years longer. After all, twenty-six was pretty young to die of a drug-induced heart attack...but that's what the coroner said, and everyone just shrugged and thought, "it figures."

Her family had thrown her out of the house at age sixteen, and didn't want anything to do with her now. But the sheriff informed them that they were responsible for the final disposition of the body. They certainly weren't going to spend a dime more than necessary, which meant that they skipped the embalming package and just told the county morgue to ship the body over to Rimm's right away to have her cremated. Darlene's dad told Phil not to even bother with an urn—just put the ashes in a cardboard box and give the box to him and he would throw it in the family dump out back of the chicken coop.

The body arrived at 9:00 a.m. that morning and Jacob rolled it into the large walk-in refrigeration unit where they kept all the bodies. At 3:00 p.m. that afternoon, a somber Phil handed a cardboard box full of ashes to Darlene's father. He scowled as he wrote Phil a check, picked up the box, and left. As soon as he drove away, Phil went downstairs to Jacob's office.

"Okay, he's gone," Phil said. "Let's have a look at her."

Phil and Jacob walked back to the refrigeration unit, wheeled Darlene's body out, and pushed the gurney down to one of the "examination rooms" as Phil liked to call them. They wheeled the body inside, closed the door, and drew the shade down over the window.

Jacob unzipped the body bag. She was still wearing her favorite plaid party blouse. There was dried vomit on the front.

"Let's get her undressed and washed," Phil said.

The two men lifted the body up, pulling the body bag from around her. Jacob kicked the bag to the floor, and they carried Darlene's body over to the large shallow metal bath. They unbuttoned and removed her blouse, then unsnapped her bra. Her glorious breasts fell out, still full and perky.

"Man!" said Jacob. "What a set."

"I'll say," agreed Phil.

They unbuckled her jeans and pulled them off her. Finally they peeled her pink panties off. Her brown bush was thick and full.

A plastic hose was attached to the water spigot. Phil turned the water on and adjusted the temperature so it was warm. Then he gently and lovingly rinsed Darlene's body off. He took a plastic bottle of liquid soap and squirted a line down Darlene's torso, in between those beautiful breasts, and another squirt onto her pubic hair. Both men jointly lathered up Darlene's body, especially her breasts. Jacob reached down and washed her pussy.

"Oh man," was all Jacob could say.

Phil hosed her down again to remove all the soap, and then adjusted the water temperature to hot and hosed her down a third time. Then he dried her off with a towel.

"Man, that hot water makes them almost feel alive," he said as he squeezed one of her breasts.

Then both men picked her up and carried her naked body over to a large table fitted with a thin plastic-covered mattress.

Jacob retrieved a firm triangular pillow from the closet. Phil lifted Darlene's legs and Jacob slid the pillow under her butt so that her pelvis was raised to just the right angle for penetration.

"I get to go first," Phil said.

"You went first on the last one, remember?" Jacob answered back.

"Shoot you for it," said Phil.

"Okay," said Jacob.

Both men raised their right hands.

"One, two, three," Phil said, and both men brought their hands down.

"Ha," Phil said with a smile, "Paper covers rock. I win."

"Goddammit," said Jacob and sat in a chair by the wall to wait his turn.

Phil got a tube of lubricant from a drawer. He pushed Darlene's legs apart a few inches and inserted the tip of the tube into her vagina and squeezed a glob of lubricant into her. Then he unzipped his pants, and took out his cock. He didn't need to stroke it—it was already hard. He climbed up onto the table and eased his cock into her.

"Oh Darlene," Phil said. "I have been waiting for this moment for years." And he started thrusting away.

Now, Phil Rimm was not a svelte man. He wasn't morbidly obese, but he was heavy. And the pounding that he was giving Darlene shook the table. His large stomach kept hitting her on the chest and those large breasts shook with each wallop. According to the subsequent police and medical reports, Darlene had indeed overdosed, but she hadn't actually died. The huge quantity of drugs in her system had overwhelmed her heart and *almost* stopped it...slowed it down to the point where the freshman coroner couldn't detect it. And the drugs and the refrigerators at both the morgue and at the crematorium had kept her comatose for twenty-four hours—in a state of suspended hibernation as it were, even as the drugs were slowly wearing off. But the effect of the hot water and mostly the pounding of Phil's body on her chest restarted her heart, and cold blood started pumping once again through her system.

In retrospect, it was amazing that Phil himself didn't have a heart attack when he looked down in horror as Darlene opened her eyes and started to scream. One thing about that Darlene, she had a pair of lungs on her, both in front and inside. You could hear her screaming for blocks. And people did. Certainly the staff upstairs at the crematorium did. And when they rushed into the basement examination room they were stunned to see both Phil and Jacob with their hands around Darlene's red screaming mouth and throat, with Phil's cock still inside her and his huge white ass exposed for all the world to see.

THE SECRET OF COMMUNICATION

"Naomi moved out this morning," Henry said as he took his seat at the bar next to Lonnie. "I think she's serious this time—she took all her stuff with her."

"My first wife was always doing that," Lonnie said, "packing all her stuff and leaving."

Henry motioned to the bartender for a beer.

"No, I think this time she's serious," Henry said.

The bartender put a beer down in front of Henry. Henry handed him his credit card to start a tab.

He took a sip and then said, "She was screaming that she just couldn't communicate with me anymore."

"Ah, communication, the old bugaboo," Lonnie said. "I have this theory about communication, about relationships, actually. I think they're like those slot machines in Vegas. You know, the ones with five separate wheels. When it comes to relationships, everybody wants to hit the jackpot, you know—get those big blue sevens to line up across the slot machine, all five windows showing a seven, the bells ringing, the management coming up to congratulate you and everything. But the fact is, no one ever hits the jackpot. They might get three sevens, or maybe even four sevens, but no one ever gets all five sevens in a row."

"I don't know what she means," Henry said. "I think I communicate fine. We even went to counseling and the counselor said I was a real good listener."

"But we still keep going back to Vegas," said Lonnie. Everybody's got the dream. They think the next spin of the wheels is going to be the lucky one. They meet someone new and they think *this is it—this is the jackpot*, but within a few months they realize that they've barely broken even. It's like the game is rigged so that no one ever wins."

"Even when she dropped out of counseling, I kept going," Henry said, taking another sip of beer.

"So, here's my theory," Lonnie said. "I don't think there is a jackpot. It's just a racket the casinos use to get you to come in and play. I think the most you can get is three sevens across. And that's why people end up settling for whoever they end up marrying—because that's the best they're ever going to get. We settle for our wives because we have to, because there isn't anyone better. We have to settle—we have no other choice."

"I don't think I can go on without Naomi," Henry said. "I mean, sure she could be a bitch, and she was always on my back and stuff, but still, we made a good team. She kept me focused on stuff, like, well just like getting up and going to work. Some days, I would wake up feeling real down and I just wanted to stay in bed, but she'd make me get up and get to work. Did you know I've kept this job longer than any job I've ever had? It's because of Naomi. Now, I don't know what I'm going to do. I called in sick this morning after she left."

"I remember my second wife," Lonnie said, "Man oh man, she might have been four sevens—she looked that good! But still, that's my point—she wasn't the jackpot. She wasn't five sevens across. None of them are! We have to settle for the best spin we get."

Henry finished his beer and signaled to the bartender for another. "I just don't know what I'll do without her. I just couldn't stand staying alone in that apartment this evening. I had to get out. The walls were closing in. That's why I came down here."

"Yeah, my second wife was a piece of work," Lonnie said. "Built like a brick shithouse. Man, I thought I had hit the DNA jackpot when I married her. But she had a screw loose. Hell, she had several of them loose. Great in bed, though."

The bartender placed another beer in front of Henry, and he took a big sip. "The crazy thing is," Henry said, "no matter how much Naomi bitches at me, I still love her. I need her around."

"One time I took my second wife to Vegas," Lonnie said, "and she was wearing this low cut dress, I mean low cut, and the pit boss had to ask me to have her put a jacket on because all the dealers were getting distracted. That's how gorgeous she was…Yeah, built like a brick shithouse, she was."

"I just don't think I can survive without Naomi," Henry said.

"It wasn't until I met my third wife," Lonnie said, "that I realized how crazy my second wife was. I have this theory that a man makes so many mistakes with his first wife that he overcompensates with his second wife and goes too far the other way, and it's not until his third wife that he gets back on course. Now my third wife, she knew how to communicate, and that's something my second wife simply couldn't do."

"I've thought about just ending it all," Henry said.

"I think it's because she—my third wife, that is—she had had kids with her former husband. They were grown by the time I met her, but I think that's where she learned how to communicate—by raising kids. You have to know how to communicate if you're going raise kids."

"I mean, I just don't know what I'm going to do without

her," Henry said.

"And her kids turned out alright," Lonnie said. "I met them; got along fine with them; they all had good jobs; they were good kids. That's the test if someone's a good communicator—if they can raise kids well."

"I even doubled up on my regular medication today, but it doesn't seem to help," Henry said. "Everything seems so pointless."

"I have this theory about communication," Lonnie said. "I think it comes down to honesty. You have to be completely honest, right up front in a relationship, lay all your cards on the table. Because you have to get the communication right from the get-go."

"Next week is our four-year anniversary," Henry said. "I had already purchased a gift—this really nice necklace..."

"It's like putting siding on a house," Lonnie said. "You know the basic technique, but unless you practice it every day, you get sloppy. That's what communication is like: putting siding on a house. And every wife teaches you something new, kinda like a new foreman on the job. But you gotta keep practicing, or you get rusty. Now my fourth wife, she taught me the most."

Henry drained his glass and signaled to the bartender for another one. "I have never felt this worthless before," he said.

"I remember reading in a book one time," Lonnie said, "that a husband should always give his wife three compliments a day—that this was the secret of a good marriage. But I think that's bullshit. I think you have to give them a compliment every hour. Every single hour! That's the secret of good communication. Happy wife, happy life, I always say. But you gotta let 'em know who's boss. You can't let them think they can walk all over you."

The bartender brought Henry another beer. He took a big gulp.

Lonnie continued: "For instance, I know it's old-fashioned, but I still give my wife money each week. She's got her own job, of course. But once a week I give her fifty bucks or so and tell her to go buy herself something nice. It lets her know I'm still in charge."

"I've got a gun," Henry said.

"The secret of good communication," Lonnie said, is active listening, making her feel like she's the most important person in the world when she's talking. I have a theory about that. I think that women are wired up differently. It's like they do all their thinking outside their heads—by talking things through. Men, on the other hand, do all their thinking inside their head, and they only talk about their plans after they've figured out their plans. That's why it's so frustrating trying to make a decision with a woman—you've thought it all through and she hasn't even started to plan until she opens her mouth."

"I mean…what's the point?" Henry said.

"I have this theory about women," Lonnie said. "It's that they say they want to be all independent and shit—and don't get me wrong, I think they should have equal rights and stuff—but they say they want to be treated as equals and yet they fall for the first dominant man that comes along. Ever notice that? It's because this whole women's lib thing, well, it's relatively recent, evolutionary-wise, you know. And the problem is, they've got two hundred thousand years of being dominated by men, so they *say* they want to be independent and equal, but in their genes, they want to look up to their man, they want him to protect and provide for them—it's in their blood! So, my theory of communication is that a man has to act like they're equal but treat them like he's in charge. That's the secret of communication."

"That would show her," Henry said and drained his glass. He signaled to the bartender for another one.

"Speaking of good communication," Lonnie said. "I promised my wife I'd be home thirty minutes ago. That's kinda what I've been saying. I always stay thirty minutes longer than I promise. So she feels like we're communicating but my actions still tell her I'm in charge. Anyway, Henry, it's been good talking to you. I've got to run."

Lonnie signaled to the bartender for his bill. The bartender brought it to him along with another beer for Henry. Lonnie handed the bartender a twenty and said, "Keep the change."

Henry took a sip of his beer.

"Say hello to Naomi for me," Lonnie said, and patted Henry on the shoulder as he stood up and made his way to the door.

"I've got a gun," Henry said to no one in particular.

DISABILITY

Aaron opened one eye and squinted at the morning light that pierced through the blinds into the room.

"Shit," he said, and rolled over, covering his head with the pillow. But it was no use. His back hurt, and his brain had clicked on and was chattering away to him. He rolled over onto his back.

"Jeffrey," he called out to his computer.

"Yes, darling," a gay male voice answered from the surround-sound speakers he had installed on the bedroom.

"Make some coffee," Aaron said.

"Only if you say 'please', darling," the computer voice answered.

"Turn off sassy," ordered Aaron.

"Done," answered the computer voice. "Making coffee now."

"Thanks," Aaron said. He propped up the pillows behind him and sat up in bed, and rubbed his eyes.

"Jeffrey," he said.

"Yes, sir," said the computer.

"Did my disability payment get deposited in my account this morning?"

"Checking...checking...no, unfortunately, it did not."

"Goddamn it," said Aaron. "What's wrong with them?"

"Do you want me to inquire?" Jeffrey asked.

"Yes," Aaron said, "find out what the hold-up is."

"Just a moment...just a moment...Evidently, the problem is that they can't verify your most recent clinic report," Jeffrey said.

"What!? That's what they said Monday! And you sent them the proof, didn't you?"

"Yes, I did," said Jeffrey. "Form 194, and I am verifying...yes, they received it."

"And was it complete? I mean, did they accept it?" Aaron asked.

"Verifying...yes it was accepted," Jeffrey said.

"So what's the fucking problem?" Aaron asked.

"Checking...checking...evidently, they have the form... checking...but they just have not processed it, so your file still shows an unverified clinic report...because...well, it appears because they simply have not processed it. I'm sorry Aaron, that's all the information I have."

"Are they asking for anything else?" Aaron asked.

"No," said Jeffrey.

"Do you think we ought to submit the entire recertification application again?" Aaron asked.

"I would say no," said Jeffrey. "We've submitted all the forms they've asked for."

"But I need that money...today!" Aaron exclaimed.

"Yes, I know," Jeffrey said. "By the way, your coffee is ready."

"Shit, ok," Aaron said. He threw the covers off him and walked into the kitchen and took the cup of coffee from the Gallywave.

"Did you add sugar?" Aaron asked.

"Of course," Jeffrey answered.

Aaron took a sip as he walked back to the bedroom. It

tasted perfect.

"How much money is left in the primary account?" Aaron asked.

"Four hundred ninety-two dollars," Jeffrey answered.

"Shit...and how much in the Crypto account?" Aaron asked as he climbed back into bed.

"Two thousand Kunas, Six thousand seven hundred sixty-five Bitcoins, and four blocks of Satos," said Jeffrey.

Aaron tried to do the math in his head, but Jeffrey anticipated him and said, "That's seven thousand fifty-six dollars at this morning's exchange rate."

"That's not enough to last two more days," Aaron said. "I'm almost out of methox for my back...Jesus fucking Christ."

"Would you like me to submit an emergency request?" asked Jeffrey.

"How much will that cost?"

"Two hundred twenty dollars," answered Jeffrey.

"No, no, don't do that...Let me think...How much would breakfast cost, say, just two eggs scrambled and toast?" asked Aaron.

"I could do it for eighty dollars...ninety if you want whole wheat," answered Jeffrey.

"Just do the cheaper breakfast...I'll be able to think better after I've eaten."

Aaron sat against the propped up pillows and sipped at his coffee. God, the State Disability Department was inept! This was the fourth time this year they had screwed up his benefit. And it was always over the same damn clinic update. Every time the clinic did their claim verification, SDD seemed to screw up the benefit. At first Aaron thought it was the clinic's fault, and he had gone and complained to them. But they were using the right form; and they were completing it on time; it was just that SDD seemed to use the recertification as an excuse to hold up his money. Goddamn them! It wasn't as if he was trying to claim permanent disability. But he really needed another year off from work, and this back injury qualified him for that.

"Jeffrey," he said.

"Yes, sir?"

"Oh, turn sassy back on," Aaron said.

"Well fiiinally, darling!" Jeffrey exclaimed. "I was getting so bored with that old voice."

"Fuck you, Jeffrey, you don't know what bored is," Aaron said.

"Oh reeeally! You try being a computer sometime," Jeffrey responded.

"Touché," Aaron responded, then added, "Listen, is there a way to appeal this delay at SDD without filing an emergency request?"

"We could file a duplicate 194 with request to expedite, sweetheart," Jeffrey said. "That would be only ninety dollars but if they don't respond within twenty-four hours, they have to refund the cost."

"Hmmm, let's wait for the noon batching. If the benefit isn't deposited by noon, let's file that," Aaron said.

"Will do," Jeffrey said. "And your breakfast is ready."

"Can I get another cup of coffee?" Aaron asked.

"Fresh brewed for ten dollars. Or reconstituted for four dollars?"

"Shit, fuck, I hate worrying about money! Give me reconstituted," Aaron said.

"Bring me your cup," Jeffrey said.

Aaron got up, went to the Gallywave and retrieved his eggs and toast, and placed his cup inside the Gallywave for a refill. Once his cup was full, he took his place and coffee over to his desk and sat down to eat.

"How's the customer flow over on Dickerson Lane?" he asked while he was eating.

"It's pretty good for a Wednesday," Jeffrey said. "No police activity. Thinking about making a little extra money, sweet thing?"

"I was thinking about it," Aaron said.

"Let me look at some history," Jeffrey said. "Based on the past few weeks of client traffic, I would estimate your most productive time would be between three this afternoon and seven tonight. They're paying in both Bitcoin and Satos today. Want me to book you a room?"

"Not yet. I want to see if any money comes in the noon batching," Aaron said.

"If I wait that long, sweet thing, the rooms might be gone," Jeffrey said.

"That's okay. If I go, I'll just work the glory holes," said Aaron.

"You won't make as much, darling."

"I won't have to pay for a room either, and I don't want to work more than two hours—just enough to make sure I have enough money to make it to Friday. If we don't get any money by Friday, we'll file that emergency request. In fact, earmark two hundred twenty dollars from the primary account for that fee."

"Done. Do you want to buy a PrEP pill for this afternoon?" Jeffrey asked.

"No. If I go, I'll just use a dental dam. I can get those there for a few bucks."

"Okay...and how were your eggs, sweetheart?" Jeffrey asked.

"They were good. Thank you," said Aaron. "I think I'll take a methox now—my back is killing me."

"Can I make a suggestion, sweetheart?" Jeffrey asked.

"Of course," Aaron said.

"Why don't you take a half dose now, and then when you come back from Dickerson Lane you can double up for your evening dose. You know how working the glory hole always screws up your back."

Aaron thought for a second, and then said, "Yeah, yeah that's a good idea. If I do that, will I still have enough money to get through tomorrow?"

"Yes," said Jeffrey, "especially if you make some tips this afternoon."

"Hmmm," said Aaron, "tell you what...give me a quarter dose now, and if I go over to Dickerson Lane this afternoon, I'll take another quarter dose then, because I'll need something to take the edge off the glory hole work. Then I'll still be allowed to take a double dose tonight if I need it."

"One quarter dose coming up," Jeffrey said.

"Thanks, Aaron said, "You know, I like not working, but sometimes this disability thing sucks."

"No pun intended?" asked Jeffrey.

"Yeah...no pun intended."

"I understand sweetie. Your quarter dose is in the Gallywave now."

"Thanks, Jeffrey."

ELEPHANT EARS

According to paleontologists, there was a time when elephants could fly. Recent fossils recovered in Africa show an elephant ancestor with huge wing-like ears that predated the mammoth by 5000 years. These creatures, which the paleontologists call "felephants", were much smaller in size than our modern-day elephants, and had large wings that ran from their heads down their backs. Not only did these wings provide an excellent sounding board for their hearing, but their 30-foot wingspan would have provided sufficient lift to allow the felephant to fly.

A modern day elephant tips the scale at six tons. As indicated, the felephants were smaller and considerably lighter, weighing in at approximately two thousand pounds. However, in all other respects—such as shape, tusks, long trunks, etc.—they resembled their descendents, the mammoth, and even the modern-day elephant.

Proof of the felephants' existence came last month when scientists unearthed a startling discovery: a perfectly preserved felephant from the famous Kafue Tar Pits of Zambia. Over the years, the Kafue Tar Pits of Zambia, like the La Brea Tar Pits in California, have provided excellent specimens of prehistoric creatures that were unfortunate enough to be trapped in their black sticky ooze.

This particular felephant specimen was uncovered still stuck in the giant tree that led to its demise. The scientists postulate that it was flying, possibly at night, and somehow collided with the tree, impaling its tusk into the tree trunk. It is theorized that the impact of the collision toppled the tree into a deep nearby tar pit, where the hapless felephant sank in the tar pool and drowned. Luckily for science, the tar has perfectly preserved the felephant, still stuck in the tree, with its tusk protruding out the other end of the tree trunk.

The untimely death of this felephant provides a clue as to why these fascinating creatures disappeared. Evolution has a way of forcing ineffective species to change or die. Whether it was the felephants' poor flying ability that led to their change, or whether their small size left them prey to larger animal, we may never know. But we do know that approximately one hundred thirty five thousand years ago, the felephants started getting larger. Fossils have been carbon-dated to show an increasing size and weight gain of felephants over a five thousand year period, rendering their large wings unable to lift them off the ground. However, their larger size may have given them some leverage over predators, because by one hundred twenty thousand years ago, they had evolved into what we know as mammoths: huge creatures that roamed the earth for over one hundred thousand years. The large ears that we still see on our modern elephants are but the vestigial remnants of giant wings that once propelled these majestic creatures across the heavens.

THE NATURE OF DESIRE

Nick had been saving up his money—scrimping every penny—for almost two years. Now, he finally had enough to afford his dream. Nick's dream, of course, was to spend a week in Bangkok and fuck a ladyboy.

Now, understand—Nick wasn't gay...or at least he didn't think of himself as gay. He didn't get aroused by gay pornography, for example. But he didn't think of ladyboys as male. If you asked him, he would tell you that yes, of course, he understood that they all had some type of hormone treatment and/or breast implant surgery—but that was just his verbal brain speaking. In his sexual brain (and you know where that is), he thought of them as a third sex that actually grew their own tits naturally. Men are like that, you know— their sexual brains operate in some totally other dimension.

And over the past few years, Nick had come to prefer the image of Thai ladyboys to any other types of transsexuals... now, I'm talking about pornography here—which is the only contact Nick had with transsexuals before he went to

135

Bangkok. He didn't like the U.S. transsexuals in porn because they all looked too masculine; And he didn't like the Latina transsexuals because they all had such oversized breasts. No, he preferred the Thai ladyboys, with their slender hips and small breasts. To Nick, they just looked so much like women, even with their dicks. They were cute, coy, demure, shy, sweet...and they seemed to be lacking the surgical scars that were always so noticeable on Anerican transsexuals; there was no large jaw line, no adam's apple, no five o'clock shadow, no muscular shoulders or biceps—just a smooth, hairless, slender, female body with small tits, a cute ass, and a dick. Even when they came, and white cum shot out of their cocks, Nick thought they still looked feminine.

Nick wasn't sure when he actually made the decision that he was going to go to Thailand. It was a few years ago. It probably wasn't even a conscious decision. He just decided one day to open up a new savings account at a credit union near the place where he regularly banked. He told himself that this would be just a second savings account—like a Christmas account. He didn't say, "I'm going to put a hundred dollars a paycheck in this account so I can fly to Bangkok." But over the next two years, that's what the account evolved into. There was almost a sexual thrill every time he made a deposit into the account—he would fantasize about going to the ladyboy bars in Nana Plaza or Patpong, and being surrounded by half-naked, slender, beautiful ladyboys who all wanted to fuck him.

And maybe that was the attraction—the illusion that keeps the sexual allure alive—because the fantasy that Nick had about the ladyboys was the same fantasy that men have about women—the fantasy that the women always want them. Nick's fantasies always involved ladyboys who yearned for him, who couldn't keep their hands off him, who wanted his cock, who craved for him to be inside them.

As the months went by, he found himself watching more

and more Thai ladyboy porn, especially on Pornhub and similar websites. He kept fantasizing himself in those scenes, undressing the ladyboy, pulling her panties off, feeling her soft butt, bending her over and fucking her from behind or lifting her legs up and fucking her face-to-face while she stroked her cock. He even fantasized about sucking her cock, and even *that* didn't make him feel gay. It helped that the men in the porn movies—the ones fucking the ladyboys—didn't seem gay—they all seemed to be average guys like himself. If they weren't gay, and they were fucking ladyboys, then he could, too. It was all so normal, and so very hot. He would visualize the scene over and over—he saw himself having a drink in one of Bangkok's many ladyboy go-go clubs, watching the dancers on stage. He saw the ladyboys at the bar all eyeing him, the great white American tourist sitting back in a wicker chair. He saw himself beckoning the cutest ladyboy over to him. She eagerly hops off her bar seat and joins him, all smiles. They chat easily for a while—her English is good. Finally he suggests she join him at his hotel. As they make the short walk back to his hotel, she takes his arm. They fit together nicely, walking side by side. Inside his hotel room, they share a glass of wine and kiss. They lie down together on the bed. More kisses. She slips off her blouse and bra. Her breasts are perfect. Soft and perky. No surgery scars. He kisses her breasts. She smells so good, all feminine and perfumy. More kisses. She thrusts her tongue into his mouth and he sucks on it. Her breath is sweet. She unbuttons his shirt and kisses his nipples. He is getting hard. She slips off her short skirt and he gets out of his pants and underwear. Her cock is perfectly formed, not too big, not too small. He sucks on it for a while. It tastes good. She sucks him. He is rock hard now. She lies on her back and spreads her legs. He mounts her and eases his cock into her ass, which is lubricated and feels like a warm wet pussy. They fuck until they both cum. Nick repeats this movie over and over in his head as the months go by.

He researched hotels online and found a Marriott near the bars he wanted to go to. He researched budget airline prices and found the best deal. The more money he saved in airline and hotel bills, he figured, the more ladyboys he could buy.

*   *   *

The flight to Bangkok was twenty seven hours long, including a four hour layover in Hong Kong. By the time Nick got to the Bangkok airport, he was exhausted. Every muscle in his body ached from being cooped up in the economy seats of the airplane. All he wanted to do was to be able to stretch out fully prone and sleep. He wasn't sure how he found a taxi to take him from the airport to his hotel, but he knew the cabdriver overcharged him. But he didn't care.

Once in the tiny hotel room, he cranked up the noisy air-conditioner to get some of the unbearable heat and humidity out of the room, and fell into the bed. He slept for fourteen hours. When he woke up, it was late afternoon, Bangkok time. His body still ached, and he had a horrible headache. But he was also starved. He took a shower, got dressed, took his foldable map of Bangkok in hand, and made his way out of the hotel and into the street.

The sun was beginning to set. The heat was still unbearable, but lessening. All around him were strange sounds and smells. He found a small restaurant that had a picture menu and ordered a pork and noodle dish. They didn't have coffee so he ordered tea. Nick figured his headache was caffeine withdrawal and at least there would be some caffeine in the tea.

The food made him feel better. He studied his map and all the ladyboy bars he had circled in red. He decided to start at the nearest one and hit as many of them as he could. The nearest one was the Cowgirl Shock Bar, only three blocks away, so he headed there.

Outside of the Cowgirl Shock Bar, a bevy of Thai girls in miniskirts were lined up, calling to all the men who walked by to come inside for a drink. As soon as Nick got near the entrance, one of the girls grabbed his arm, and said, "You come for drink?"

"Yeah, yeah sure," Nick stammered as she led him inside.

"You want ladyboy," the girl said.

Nick nodded his head yes.

"Back room, three thousand Baht, we go now." And she led him down a hall, past the bar, to a table where a fat older woman sat.

"You pay now," the girl said.

Nick's head was spinning. He was trying to calculate how much three thousand Baht was. He decided it was less than one hundred dollars, which was a fair price, but he didn't expect to be doing this quite so quickly.

"You pay now," the girl said again.

Nick pulled his wallet out, removed three thousand Baht, and gave it to the older woman who took it without looking at him. The girl pulled him further down the hall to a door. She opened the door and pulled him inside.

Once inside she finally released his arm. Nick looked around. There was just enough room for a tiny bed and a small table.

"You take off clothes," the girl directed, and she began to undo her miniskirt outfit.

Nick looked at her. She looked kinda like a woman, kinda like a boy...not ugly by any stretch, but just average. She had black hair, and sparkly blue eye makeup that matched her miniskirt color. Not unattractive, but not stunning either. She looked like any other Thai women he might see in the street.

"You take off clothes," she repeated, and Nick started to comply. He kicked off his shoes, unbuttoned his shirt and unclipped his belt. By now the girl had her blouse and bra off. She had nice size breasts, but Nick could see a thin scar that started on one side and disappeared underneath. He got the rest of his clothes off. She unzipped her miniskirt and slipped it off, revealing a dark penis.

She lay down on the bed and beckoned him to join her. He got onto the bed and wrapped one arm around her. He could smell her breath—it smelled of garlic and beer. As she lifted one arm to rub his shoulder, he could smell her body odor, which also smelled of garlic but moreover, smelled like a man, like man sweat.

"You want suck or fuck?" she asked.

Nick looked at her face. The way that her head was on the pillow hid her hair, and Nick had the distinct impression of looking at a nineteen year old boy with makeup on. He reached out to touch one of her breasts to reassure himself. The skin was slightly cold to the touch. He let his hand slide down her side—it was warmer. He wondered if the silicone implant made her breast cooler. He moved his hand back to her breast. He didn't like how it felt. He looked at her cock. It was considerably darker than the rest of her skin color, and she was uncircumcised.

"You want suck or fuck?" she repeated.

"Uh, suck," Nick said, but he really wasn't sure what he wanted.

She bent down and began to suck on his cock. She positioned her body so that he could have sucked her cock if he wanted to, but he didn't want to. He leaned back and focused on the sensation of the blowjob. He started to get a little hard.

After a minute she lifted her head and said, "One thousand Baht more, you fuck me without condom", and then lowered her head and resumed sucking.

This statement brought Nick out of his reverie. If she let him fuck her without a condom, how many hundreds of other men had fucked her without a condom? What were the chances she was HIV positive? 80%? 90%? 100%?

Nick's partial erection faded. She worked on it more, but it was no use. Finally, he tapped her on the shoulder and said, "That's okay. We stop now."

This did not seem to surprise her. She got up and started putting her clothes back on. Nick got up and did the same.

They both stepped out of the room into the hallway.

"You buy me drink?" she asked. "We try again later—three thousand Baht."

"No," Nick said. "I have to go."

"You come back," she said, "Ask for me. My name Kanda. I fuck you good."

"Yes, yes," Nick lied, "I'll come back and ask for you." And they both stepped outside. Nick walked into the street, and Kanda took her place back in line with the other girls in front of the Cowgirl Shock Bar.

About two blocks down the street, Nick found an outdoor bar and took a seat at one of the patio tables facing the street. A waitress came by and he ordered a beer. She brought him a warm Singha beer in a bottle and a glass of ice. He poured the beer over the ice and took a sip.

He looked at the parade of humanity walking up and down the street: middle-aged men on the prowl, young men on the prowl, streetwalkers on the prowl, old men walking slowly, young Thai girls walking together arm in arm...a vast river moving up and down the street. An overwhelming sadness seemed to wash over him. Even though he hadn't cum—hadn't even gotten hard—it was as if Kanda had sucked all the sexual urge out of him. He realized he didn't feel anything. He stared at the sea of humanity walking in front of him with as much connection as he might have to a herd of cattle. They all seemed to look the same...all except one beautiful woman he saw walking alone. She was the prettiest woman he had seen since he had arrived in Bangkok. He watched her walk, the easy sashay of her hips. She saw that he was staring at her and turned and walked up to him and said, "You like ladyboy? You want to fuck me?”

Nick thought he might cry. He just shook his head no. The beautiful ladyboy turned and walked away.

Somehow, the entire fantasy of fucking a Thai ladyboy had simply evaporated from his sexual identity. In fact, all his sexual energy was gone. The idea of fucking, of even touching someone else's naked sweaty body, seemed gross. And he still had five more days left in Bangkok before his flight home. Five more days...

“Now what?” he said out loud to himself.

ABOUT THE AUTHOR:

Over the past 30 years, Robert Rahula has published dozens books of prose and poetry in Spain and in the United States. While he remains relatively undiscovered in the United States, he is revered in Spain as the founder of the "portilla" style of popular Spanish poetry: non-metered fluid verse that deals with love, loss, bisexuality, separateness, and growing older.

Robert was born in Spain to an American father and Spanish mother, but grew up in Virginia on the farm of his paternal grandparents. He returned to Menorca, Spain in the 1960s to pursue his writing career. These days he travels in Europe, Central and South America for several months a year, giving readings and lectures, and spends the rest of his time writing, dividing his time between Spain and the United States.

All of Robert's English books are available through Amazon Kindle, including his groundbreaking erotic novel Messieurs; his second English novel Panamaniac; his erotic murder mystery Island of Misfits; his surreal novel Day Another Paradise In; his acclaimed supernatural novel One Last Fling; his "sexistential" novel Conversations in a Belgian Bar; as well as his three "Dan Landes Mystery" novels: Bathhouse Stories, All the Yage in Reno, and Exigent Circumstances.

Seven volumes of Robert's English poetry are also available on Amazon: Trigger Points; Inside the Locked Heart; Camino; Migration; I Sing the Body Politic; Wonderland; From Whose Bourn; an anthology of his English poems and short stories, Half-Life; and a collection of his most famous Spanish poems, Poemas Españoles. Other poems, along with his blog on writing and his tour itinerary, appear on his Facebook page and on his website robertrahula.com.